Guardians of the Keystones

Ed Morgan

Guardians of the Keystones

In memory of
David Walker Day
5/23/23 - 10/24/24
Gone too soon

CONTENTS

DEDICATION   v

2   Guardians of the Keystones: Echoes   25

3   Guardians of the Keystones: Echoes   36

4   Guardians of the Keystones: Echoes   47

5   Guardians of the Keystones: Echoes   63

6   Guardians of the Keystones: Echoes   74

7   Guardians of the Keystones: Echoes   83

8   Guardians of the Keystones: Echoes   93

9   Guardians of the Keystones: Echoes   106

10   Guardians of the Keystones: Echoes   114

11   Guardians of the Keystones: Echoes   124

12   Guardians of the Keystones: Echoes   137

13   Guardians of the Keystones: Echoes   147

14   Guardians of the Keystones: Echoes   159

Pronunciations   174

15   Acknowledgments   175

ABOUT THE AUTHOR   176

Guardians of the Keystones: Echoes

Chapter One

My name is Arkeia, and I am a whisperer from a time long past, a living echo of a world swallowed by legend. It was eons ago, so many years before the gnawing hunger of time began its feast, when I was chosen. The Elder Gods themselves, their forms shifting like nebulae, selected me to be their chronicler—to bear witness to their ancient history and the cataclysmic war that even then stirred on the horizon.

I can barely recall those simpler days, a time when my spirit was untroubled by the weight of a dying age. I knew nothing then of the wonders I would see, the horrors I would record, or the profound loneliness that would become my constant companion. I began my life in Elyria, a name now lost to the vast, swirling currents of time and space. Born before its fading, I was one of the Keepers of Whispers, an ancient order dedicated to the meticulous preservation of Elyria's true history, its intricate lore, and, most crucially, its profound connection to the cosmic energies that hummed beneath its foundations. From birth, I was graced with gifts from the Elder Gods—a sensitivity to the ebb and flow of time and space, and a perfect, unwavering memory for every detail presented to me.

These were blessings that would, in time, become both my greatest strength and my heaviest burden.

Elyria was a city of breathtaking beauty, a living tapestry woven with vibrant hues. Its gardens were a kaleidoscope of colors unseen elsewhere in the galaxy, each bloom a silent symphony. Our home planet, Vestara, was blessed by twin suns that graced our eastern horizon, one after the other. Their rising was a spectacle of celestial artistry, washing the skies with deep, ethereal blues that bled into fiery, passionate reds, painting the vast silver grass fields below. In the cool morning breeze, the fields would shimmer, a million tiny mirrors reflecting the nascent light. As the suns climbed, the echo weavers would begin their song. Faint at first, a delicate hum on the wind, their melody would swell, building into a powerful chorus that drifted for miles. Their voices, blending and harmonizing with others, created a symphony of unparalleled beauty, a sound that resonated deep within the soul of every Elyrian. It truly was the most beautiful city in the galaxy, a testament to peace and harmony.

High above, perched upon the Great Mountain, stood the Citadel. Here, the leaders of our realm convened, their wisdom guiding the fragile peace throughout the known universe. At its heart lay the Resonant Orb, an enigmatic relic whose true purpose had been lost to the annals of time, whispered to be as ancient as creation itself. But deeper still, rumored to lie within the heavily guarded catacombs beneath the Citadel, was another, even older relic: the Prime Keystone. This artifact, predating the multiverse, held immense, forgotten power and magic, a silent pulse at the very core of our world.

Elyria. The very name, a melody upon the tongue, conjures the image of a city cradled in the arms of giants. It was unlike any other metropolis my aged eyes have witnessed. Nestled in a verdant valley, Elyria was a jewel box embraced by the towering shoulders of twin mountains, their peaks piercing the heavens themselves. Seven rolling hills formed the heart of this haven, a vibrant tapestry woven with bustling markets overflowing with the bounty of the land, and homes nestled within high, protective walls, like children gathered at their mother's skirts. For countless centuries, this tranquil land flourished, a sanctuary of balance and peace where time itself seemed to flow at a gentler pace, a lullaby whispered on the mountain winds.

The first souls to settle this fair city were not mere settlers; they were the Sentinels, beings tasked by the Elder Gods with a sacred duty: to watch over the Prime Keystone. They chose this valley, nestled between the two great mountains, not only for its breathtaking beauty or natural defensibility, but because the mountains themselves acted as natural conduits, channeling and grounding the immense, latent power radiating from the Prime Keystone, hidden deep beneath the earth. Over millennia, drawn by the palpable sense of peace and harmony emanating from the valley, others arrived. The city of Elyria grew organically around the Sentinels' hidden work, blossoming into a place of breathtaking beauty, nurtured by the unique environment of Vestara.

Elyrian society evolved under the subtle, passive influence of the Keystone's presence. Peace wasn't merely a policy; it was an ambient state, the very air we breathed. Art and music, largely inspired by the ethereal songs of the echo weavers, flourished. Philosophy and historical record-keeping became paramount. The order known as the Keepers of Whispers arose from the lineage of the original Sentinels and those most sensitive to the valley's unique energies. We became the city's dedicated historians and loremasters, secretly aware of the true relic hidden beneath the city—the Prime Keystone in its sacred shrine—and the enigmatic Orb within the Citadel. We understood our sacred duty: to observe, record, and protect this profound knowledge, ensuring the city maintained the delicate balance required for the Keystone's safety, even if the general populace remained blissfully unaware of the ultimate source of their enduring peace.

Elyria's idyllic existence wasn't shattered by the ravages of war, but rather veiled by foresight. Millennia ago, as the war for control of the multiverse raged ever closer to Vestara, the Elder Gods realized the Prime Keystone's location, even hidden, was dangerously exposed. To protect it, they enacted a long, subtle ritual, intricately tied to the cycle of the twin suns and Vestara's unique dimensional properties. This wasn't a relocation; it was a gradual shifting of Elyria's entire region slightly out of phase with the primary reality stream of its universe. It became a place one could only stumble upon if specific, complex conditions were met, or if guided by immense power or knowledge. Elyria faded from maps, from memory, slowly becoming a legend, a "lost city"—shielded from the multiverse until its destined time of rediscovery. A pang, a bittersweet ache, resonates within my very soul. My own home, lost to the relentless march of years, feels a distant, fading echo. Once, it shone as the radiant gem of the Kaprius galaxy, a beacon of civilization in the cosmos.

But now, that great city, that once vibrant metropolis, exists only in the shadowed chambers of memory, swallowed by the insatiable hunger of time, a phantom kingdom in the realm of what once was. Yet, the beauty of Elyria, this haven between the peaks, offered a flicker of solace, a gentle reminder that even in the face of loss, life, like a wildflower pushing through stone, finds a way to bloom again. As Elyria became the lost city it is today, the Elder Gods saw the crucial need to chronicle the history of the Gods themselves and all of their creation. They knew there would come a time when this history would need to be shared, remembered, and never forgotten again.

I was chosen to be the living vessel of their history, a vessel of memory in a world prone to forgetting. I was placed in a Temporal Sanctuary deep within the hidden levels of the Citadel, near the very chamber of the Keystone, yet shielded from its direct, overwhelming influence. This sanctuary was a pocket of slowed time, designed to preserve me until the destined moment of rediscovery, to ensure Elyria's profound knowledge wouldn't be entirely lost to the encroaching darkness. I became a sleeper, a watcher of the multiverse, guarding the memory of a city as it fades into legend, waiting for the day my story can finally be told. This is my story.

The wind howled across the desolate plains of Sonus, a razor-edged gale that carried the biting scent of rusting metal and the heavy, undeniable presence of something profoundly ancient. It scoured the iron-rich sand, whistling through glassy, lightning-forged formations that jutted from the ground like broken teeth. Lirien of the Bramah drew his cloak tighter, the heavy fabric a futile shield against the oppressive atmosphere. This was neutral territory, a fragile ground designated for truce, yet the charged stillness felt like the moment before a blade is drawn.

A scion of the revered Bramah lineage, younger brother to their esteemed leader Aethon, Lirien had embarked on this perilous journey as a beacon of last-ditch hope. His mastery over celestial magic flowed through his veins like starlight, a power of harmony and order. His diplomat's silver tongue, honed over centuries of negotiation, was his sharpest weapon. He alone was deemed capable of attempting to forge this tenuous, desperate alliance with the enigmatic Shivara.

Across the windswept plain, Kael, their paramount leader, stood like a jagged shard of obsidian given form—an affront to the natural order. He radiated a barely contained impatience that clawed at the air, his very presence a promise of violence. Surrounding them both, their entourages formed a silent, tense circle. Bramah Sentinels, bastions of unwavering calm, stood opposite Shivara Devastators, whose coiled, predatory energy hummed beneath layers of forced discipline.

Lirien's mission was clear, though its success felt impossibly distant: to parley with Kael, to penetrate the Shivara's impenetrable resolve, and to somehow craft a truce that would stay the bloody hand of war. On these sweeping, wind-scoured plains, the two leaders met, their gazes locked, each searching for weakness, for truth, in the other.

"A truce, Kael," Lirien reiterated, his voice a smooth, practiced melody that masked the cold dread coiling in his gut. He had to make him understand. "A cessation of hostilities. We need time, Kael. Time to comprehend what truly shifts beneath our feet, before this endless conflict devours us all."

Kael scoffed, a harsh, guttural sound swallowed by the ceaseless wind. "Comprehend?" He took a step forward, the ground crunching beneath his armored boot. "The only truth in this universe, Bramah, is power. Your 'balance' is nothing but stagnation, a fear of true ascension. Why should we pause our glorious campaign when dominance, total and absolute, is finally within our grasp?"

"Because," Lirien met Kael's burning, obsidian gaze, his own conviction hardening into steel, "something else stirs. Something far older than your ambition or our Order. An ancient, dissonant chord is being struck in the heart of creation. Can you not feel it, Kael? This isn't just the tremors of our war; it's the very fabric of reality groaning under an unseen, impossible weight."

Before Kael could retort, before his caustic words could fully form, the ground beneath them began to tremble.

It was not a localized quake, not the familiar rumble of Sonus's volcanic heart, but a deeper vibration, an impossible, sympathetic thrum that resonated in their bones, in the very essence of their beings. It was a ripple through creation itself, a cosmic blasphemy. Both leaders, seasoned warriors accustomed to the chaos of battle, looked up instinctively, their eyes scanning the desolate, bruised sky, though they knew the source was impossibly distant.

Light years away, perhaps even realities away, in a forgotten shrine nestled in the heart of a nameless mountain, a Keystone, dormant since the genesis of the multiverse, awakened. It had slept for eons, the silent, inert heart of a titan. Now, it throbbed with nascent energy, its pulsations growing, a slow, building crescendo that bathed the ancient stone in an ethereal, pulsating glow. Then, with a roar that was not sound but a psychic scream of raw potential, it unleashed a torrent of unbound, primordial energy.

This cosmic shockwave reverberated across its universe, a chain reaction igniting in Keystones scattered throughout the vast, interconnected multiverse. It scoured across planets, ignited dormant leylines, and made the Void itself recoil. The very ground beneath Lirien and Kael heaved and cracked violently as the unleashed power coursed like a raging river through the essence of time and space. On Sonus, the plains fractured. In the Bramah stronghold, ancient runic wards, forged to withstand cosmic tempests, flared wildly, threatening to collapse. And within the dark, hungry expanse of the Shivara sanctuary, shadows writhed with a newfound, terrifying sentience.

Lirien felt it as a profound violation, a discordant shriek ripping through the harmonious symphony of creation he had spent his life safeguarding.

Kael felt it as a surge of pure, intoxicating power—a tantalizing and terrifying promise of untold dominance, a call to arms for the worthy.

Their fragile negotiation shattered in that instant.

"This changes nothing," Kael snarled, his eyes alight with a terrifying, covetous hunger. He turned abruptly, his cloak whipping around him like a storm cloud. "It only accelerates the inevitable." He signaled his Shivara, who dissolved into ripples of distorted space, vanishing as if they had never been.

Lirien lingered only a moment longer, the world still trembling beneath him, his mind racing to process the impossible. *The Keystones? All of them?* He sent a desperate, silent thought   a mental plea imbued with all his urgency—towards his brother. *Aethon!*

Then, he folded space himself, the familiar, violent tearing of reality around him a welcome anchor in the chaos. He raced back towards the Bramah sanctuary, his heart pounding with a rhythm that mirrored the disturbed and terrified cosmos. The multiverse held its breath, the brief, shattering tremor a chilling prelude to an unknown, colossal storm.

Silence. A profound, unsettling silence. In the heart of the Bramah stronghold, the great Nexus chamber, usually alive with the subtle, comforting whispers of the Elder Gods channeled through the Oracle crystals, was utterly, deafeningly quiet. Aethon was on one knee before the central conduit, his gauntleted hand pressed against the inert, cold crystal, his face etched with strain as he struggled for a connection that simply wasn't there.

Lirien appeared beside him, his form coalescing from shimmering light, his breathing ragged.

"Brother," Lirien's voice was tight with urgency, raw with the shock of what he had witnessed on Sonus. "Did you feel it? The disruption? That sheer, raw power?"

Aethon rose slowly, his face a mask of grave concern, the weight of a thousand years settling onto his face. "I felt it, Lirien. Like the universe itself cried out in pain." He gestured to the inert Oracles that lined the chamber, their crystalline facets dark and lifeless. "And worse... They are silent."

Lirien stared, his own dread deepening. "Silent? What do you mean?"

"The Elder Gods offer no guidance," Aethon's voice was a low, hollow ache in the dead quiet of the room. "No explanation. Not a whisper. For the first time in our history, Lirien... we are utterly alone."

Aria, chief strategist and a warrior whose calm demeanor rarely wavered, approached, her usual composure visibly ruffled, her brow furrowed with a rare and profound anxiety. "Unprecedented, Aethon," she began, her voice low and strained. "The Oracles are not merely silent. Their core resonance is... cold. Like a star that has died. It's a fundamental severance. Since the First Records began, since the dawn of our memory, They have never been entirely absent after such a profound cosmic event. What... what does this mean for us?"

"It means," Aethon said slowly, the words heavy with the burden of leadership as he stared into the lifeless Oracle crystals, "that we are navigating blind. We are adrift in a storm without a star to guide us. And the Shivara..."

"Kael felt it too," Lirien confirmed grimly, stepping to his brother's side, his voice devoid of its usual diplomat's charm. "But he did not feel the violation we did, brother. I felt his mind as the wave struck. He felt... elation. As if the universe had just handed him the very weapon he has always craved. He will see this not as a sign for caution, but as a divine validation for his path to dominance. He will strike, and soon."

"Then we must be vigilant," Aethon declared, turning from the silent conduit, his mind racing through a thousand disastrous scenarios. Threat assessments, fleet readiness, the stability of their most sacred relics, the very integrity of the Great Keystone network. "More vigilant than ever before. But without Their guidance... where do we even begin to prepare? How do we build a fortress against a darkness we cannot name?"

The silence that answered was heavy, filled with the unspoken fear of three immortal leaders facing true, terrifying uncertainty for the first time in millennia. For a long moment, Aethon's shoulders seemed to bow under the impossible weight. Then, he straightened, a fire igniting in his eyes, a flicker of defiance against the encroaching dread.

"We must have faith," he declared, his voice ringing with a newfound conviction that cut through the fear like a blade. "The Gods will provide. They have done so in the past, through trials that would have shattered lesser beings, and they will not fail us this day!" He looked from Lirien to Aria, his gaze intense, compelling. "We must trust in their ultimate plan, however inscrutable it may seem now. Their silence is not absence. It is a test—a test of our resolve, of our purpose, of the very foundation upon which we were created!"

Aria nodded, the flicker of renewed resolve in her eyes catching light from Aethon's own, acknowledging the profound truth in his words. Lirien, standing beside his brother, felt a surge of conviction echoing Aethon's unwavering belief. Aethon was right. Doubt, in this hour of cosmic uncertainty, was a luxury they could not afford, a poison that would only cripple them. Their faith in the Elder Gods, a bedrock built over eons, must remain unshaken.

"Your faith inspires us, brother," Lirien said, his voice regaining its strength. "But faith must be paired with action. What are your orders?"

"Yes," Aethon agreed, his focus now sharp as a razor's edge. "We will not wait passively in the dark." He turned to Lirien. "Brother, your skills are needed now more than ever. The Gods may be silent, but Creation still has a voice. Listen to it. Use your celestial magic to read the currents of the cosmos. Trace the echoes of this disruption back to their source. Find its epicenter. I want to know what, and where, this power originated."

He then faced Aria. "Aria, you are my strategist. Assume the worst. Assume Kael will move on our most vital and vulnerable assets. Draft new defense protocols for every major Keystone in our domain. But your primary focus will be on the unknown. Once Lirien finds the epicenter of this disturbance, I want a full tactical response plan ready to deploy. We will meet this new anomaly, whatever it is, with overwhelming force."

Finally, he activated his command comm. "Thorne, report."

Thorne's voice, though distant, was immediate and clear. *"Commander. All fleets are on high alert. Sentinel patrols have been doubled."*

"It is not enough, Thorne," Aethon commanded. "I want real-time reports from every listening post in the Void-facing sectors. If a single Shivara vessel deviates from its known patrol route by so much as a parsec, I want to know. The moment Kael moves, we will be there to meet him."

He closed the channel, the Nexus chamber once more falling into a tense, but now purposeful, silence. Hope, though guarded and fragile, still flickered—a precious flame they would now shield with vigilance, strategy, and their own unshakeable resolve in the face of an uncertain future that stretched, vast and terrifying, before them.

The silence was a tangible thing in Kael's sanctuary, a hollow, mocking void where the malevolent whispers of the Dark Gods should have been. It was an absence that felt like a pressure, a smothering weight. Even the Void energies that writhed in the great viewing portal seemed agitated, their usual slow, predatory swirl replaced by a tense, chaotic churn. Kael, the fiery leader of the Shivara, stood before it, a pillar of contained rage. He had felt the cosmic tremor, the intoxicating surge of raw, untamed power unleashed upon the universe, and had expected a command, a directive, a glorious call to war.

Instead, he was met with this... this insulting emptiness.

He stalked the chamber, a caged god radiating a furious impatience, each step a thunderclap of contained power in the suffocating silence. His fists clenched and unclenched, his knuckles white.

"They dare to be silent?" he snarled, the words venomous projectiles hurled at the unresponsive darkness. "*Now?* When the universe itself screams with new potential? Why do our Gods keep us waiting like dogs at their door?!"

"My Lord Kael," Cassius interjected from the edge of the chamber, his voice a cautious, almost inaudible tremor. He knew the danger of this moment. "To question the will of the Great Darkness... the consequences could be... absolute." He swallowed hard, the unspoken threat of divine retribution hanging heavy in the air. "I am your most devoted, most ruthless servant, my lord. I would never challenge your command. But... perhaps... a degree of patience..."

"Patience?!" Kael whirled on Cassius, his eyes blazing with a fury that could incinerate worlds, the very shadows in the room seeming to recoil from him. "You dare lecture *me* on the virtues of the weak? Patience is a leash for lesser beings, Cassius! It is the prayer of the powerless hoping the storm will pass! We *are* the storm! We are not meant to wait for the tide!" He punctuated the words with a guttural growl, a sound ripped from the depths of a predatory beast. "My authority is absolute! I will determine our response to the Gods, to our enemies, to everyone! Your place is to obey, not to question!"

"Forgive me, Master," Cassius groveled instantly, his head bowed so low it nearly touched the cold, obsidian floor. "My insolence was unforgivable. A flaw to be purged. It will not be repeated."

"The Bramah," Kael spat the name like a curse, turning his fury from his subordinate to its true target. He could feel their cloying influence, their sanctimonious Order, like a poison in the cosmos. "I know they are behind this. Scheming, plotting, always worming their way into the affairs of their betters, trying to cage power they are too cowardly to wield. We should be retaliating! We should be on the move, obliterating them from their gilded stronghold, reducing their pathetic, stagnant existence to superheated ash! Why this agonizing, infuriating *wait*?!" The roar echoed through the chamber, a raw expression of unbridled hatred for the cosmic stalemate they represented.

"Indeed, master," Cassius hissed, eager to redirect the storm away from himself. "Their weakness is an insult to existence itself. The Gods will surely answer our devotion soon, and then... then we shall unleash our full wrath."

Kael's burning gaze fixed once more on the empty Void outside. "When they answer," he said, his voice dropping to a low, dangerous promise, "we will not just crush the Bramah. We will erase their memory from this universe. We will wipe their sanctimonious light clean with their own blood, and show our Gods what true, untamed power really is."

The promise hung in the air, thick with malice, a testament to the burning hatred that fueled their every action, now simmering impatiently in the maddening, divine silence.

Their universe held its breath, two armies poised on the brink of war, their fates hanging in the balance of a silence that spoke louder than any thunder. The multiverse shuddered, still reeling from the activation. Time and space, once constants, now flowed like a turbulent river, its currents warped and unpredictable.

Time itself seemed to hold its breath within the Bramah stronghold. The divine silence from the Elder Gods had stretched into a deafening, hollow void, leaving their most devout servants adrift in a sea of cosmic uncertainty. In his private sanctum, Aethon stood before the grand, silent star-map, the weight of a rudderless nation on his immortal shoulders. The fury had passed, leaving behind a cold, gnawing anxiety.

Then, it came.

Not a command, not a thunderous pronouncement, but a whisper, gentle as the first light of a newborn star, that brushed against the edge of his consciousness. The voice, serene and clear, grew not in volume but in presence, blooming within his mind. With it came a vision, a window opening into a world far away, in a universe rarely touched by the direct gaze of the Elder Gods.

He saw a great metropolis, a testament to mortal ambition, but his view was drawn downward, into the perpetually dark, rain-slicked canyons between towering skyscrapers. In a forgotten alleyway, choked with refuse and despair, a young mortal girl sat huddled against the cold, indifferent stone, her small form trembling. Silent tears traced paths of clean sorrow down her grimy cheeks. She was utterly forsaken, a beacon of fear and loneliness in the uncaring night. Aethon felt a pang of confusion. Why was he being shown this singular, mortal tragedy? What could this child possibly have to do with the fate of immortals, the silence of Gods, and the cosmic storm that was gathering?

But then, his divine senses perceived more. Beneath the misery, beneath the psychic scream of the city, he felt it—a tiny, defiant spark. A pure, unquenchable light, a perfect, harmonious resonance that hummed softly from within her, a quiet song of order in a world of chaos. His breath caught. This wasn't a vision of despair. This was the answer. This was the first word from the Gods. This was *hope*.

Aethon immediately summoned Thorne, one of his most trusted generals, to his chambers. As he waited, his mind turned to the man he had called. Thorne, forged in the crucible of mortality, was unique among the Bramah's highest ranks. Aethon remembered the tales from the Great Wars, when Thorne was but a mortal commander, his world on the brink of annihilation from a critical Shivara assault. When all hope seemed lost, when even Bramah warriors faltered, this mortal had stood, rallying his people to fight alongside the divine, his valor a shining, impossible defiance. For that act, the Elder Gods had granted him what they gave to so few: a new life, an immortal existence among the Bramah he had so bravely defended. Perhaps Thorne, who had once stared into the abyss as a mortal, could shed light on this perplexing, hopeful vision.

Thorne arrived, his presence solid and reassuring. Aethon met his general's gaze, his own eyes reflecting the unsettling, yet profound, vision.

"The silence has broken, Thorne," Aethon said, his voice low but filled with a new, vibrant energy. "I have received a vision. Not of fleets, or of Kael, but of a lone mortal girl, lost in a city of shadows."

He shared the image, the feeling, the despair, and then, the crucial, hidden detail. "But within her, Thorne, there is a light. A pure, harmonious resonance unlike anything I have ever felt. A perfect note in a symphony of chaos." His eyes, now alight with dawning purpose, met Thorne's. "Could she be the key?" he mused, the words filled with wonder. "A nexus of power, perhaps, connected to the very fabric of this disturbance... or even... the Keystones?"

Thorne's tactical mind immediately grasped the implications, but his response was driven by something deeper—the memory of mortal fragility and the ferocity of mortal hope. "If the Gods have pointed us to her, Commander, then she is more than a key; she is a sign. We cannot let that light be extinguished by the darkness surrounding it. We must act swiftly." His voice grew sharp with urgency. "Shall we journey to this world? Locate this girl and bring her into our protection? We must discover what makes her so unique."

Aethon nodded, a grim, determined set to his jaw. "And quickly—before the Shivara, in their hunger for any new source of power, learn of her existence."

"The mission is clear," Thorne declared, his voice ringing with renewed purpose. He did not hesitate. He turned, his mind already selecting the members for this critical task. He would assemble a small, elite strike team, not of his most brutal warriors, but of his most steadfast and compassionate guardians. Their mission was not one of conquest or simple retrieval. It was a mission of salvation—to venture into an unknown world, to find a single, lost spark in the darkness, and to shield it, for in her light might lie the hope of them all.

As the Bramah embarked on their desperate mission, the Shivara, in their shadowed realm, concluded a ritual of dark communion. Before them materialized Tharros, a terrifying deity, the very embodiment of dominion, power, and control. His voice, a chilling resonance, revealed the Bramah's clandestine movements, their sudden interest in a forgotten backwater of the multiverse, a sector rarely touched by either the Elder Gods or their agents.

"KAEL!" The name ripped through the chamber, a sonic assault of pure, unadulterated rage. "You *dare* question your Gods?! You exist solely to serve *OUR* will!" Tharros's scowl was a black hole of fury, his eyes burning with the inferno of a thousand dying stars.

"Forgive me, my Lord!" Kael groveled, the words a desperate plea. "Disrespect was never my intent. My only desire is to be the instrument of the Gods' vengeance."

"Your *only* desire should be unquestioning obedience!" Tharros roared, the sound shaking the very foundations of the chamber. "Know your place, worm! A flick of my wrist, a mere thought, and your existence would be snuffed out like a candle in a hurricane."

Trembling, but fueled by a desperate ambition, Kael dared to speak again, his voice a carefully controlled rasp. "This... disruption, my Lord... Was it the hand of the wretched Bramah? The meddling Elder Gods? Or... a manifestation of *our* Gods' power?"

Tharros's response was a chilling wave of disdain. "This was no act of the Gods, nor of our pathetic enemies. This was... *other*. A power that dwarfs even our own. A power we *must* seize, dominate, and bend to our will!" He paused, his voice dropping to a venomous whisper. "Dispatch your most ruthless hunters. Find what the Bramah seek. Unravel this mystery. Leave no stone unturned, no secret safe. *Everything* must be known."

Tharros's gaze, a searing inferno, locked onto Kael's, piercing his very being, burning away any pretense of defiance. Kael felt his soul shrivel under that unholy scrutiny, a helpless insect pinned beneath the gaze of a wrathful god. "A *mortal*," Tharros hissed, the word a corrosive acid, dripping with utter contempt. "A fleeting, insignificant *parasite* festers at the core of this cosmic disruption. We must unearth this creature, vivisect its secrets, and expose the source of its... *unnatural* power. And then," a predatory gleam ignited in the god's eyes, "we shall *appropriate* that power. We shall forge it into a weapon, a tool of absolute domination. This... *mortal*... will become either the cornerstone of our ascendance or be utterly annihilated in the process." The unspoken threat, the promise of unimaginable suffering, hung heavy in the air, a testament to the ruthless ambition of the Dark Gods.

"It shall be done, my Lord," Kael bowed low, his mind already racing with plans of brutal efficiency.

Tharros vanished in a blinding eruption of hellfire, leaving Kael in the echoing silence, the lingering stench of sulfur a testament to the god's wrath. The encounter had shaken him, but beneath the fear, a cold, hard determination solidified. He composed himself with a visible effort, a mask of ruthless control replacing the momentary terror. Then, with a speed born of desperation and ambition, he stormed from the chamber, ready to unleash a torrent of violence and chaos upon the unsuspecting universe. The hunt had begun.

Kael summoned Vega, his most lethal assassin, her mastery of stealth, deception, and the deadly arts essential for this critical mission. Without a moment's hesitation, Vega mobilized her elite cadre of shadow warriors and vanished into the void, racing to intercept the Bramah before they could reach their intended target.

The echoing clang of Aethon's boots against the ancient, obsidian floors of the Bramah stronghold reverberated like a death knell in his troubled heart. Each step was a heavy weight, mirroring the growing dread that coiled around him like a venomous serpent. His men, his loyal soldiers who had stood by him through countless battles, now faced a fate more terrifying than any physical wound - the unknown. Their enemy, the insidious Shivara, certainly shadowed their every move, their presence a chilling phantom that seemed to seep through the very walls of the fortress.

This hunt, this desperate scramble across the cosmos, wasn't for some ancient artifact or cosmic weapon. It was for a *mortal*. One seemingly insignificant being, a fleeting spark of life amidst the infinite expanse. But appearances, as Aethon knew all too well, could be deceiving. This was no ordinary mortal. This soul, this singular existence, held the balance of their entire reality in its precarious grasp. One wrong move, one miscalculation, and the multiverse could shatter like glass, or, perhaps, be delivered from a doom so profound, so absolute, that it defied comprehension.

And the *Shivara*... They felt it too. The tremor in the fabric of existence. Though they were a universal constant, a Keystone was in play. The nature of the Keystone was still a puzzle, but that didn't stop them. With their terrifying power to warp reality itself, to twist the very threads of time and space, they were closing in. Aethon could practically feel their presence, a suffocating darkness pressing at the edges of his awareness. Their pursuit was relentless, driven by a hunger for power that was as vast and cold as the Void itself. Every second that ticked by was a gamble, a razor's edge between salvation and utter annihilation. They were not merely chasing; they were *hunting*, and the prey was the most important being in all of creation. The air itself crackled with a sense of impending doom, a silent countdown to a catastrophe that could unravel everything. What would happen when these forces that shouldn't mix, meet?

Aethon's jaw clenched, his hand instinctively going to the hilt of the energy blade strapped to his side, a faint hum vibrating from the weapon's core. Could they even hope to find her before the Shivara unraveled the secrets of her existence? Before they twisted her power to their own wicked ends? The task felt monumental, a dizzying precipice overlooking an abyss of despair. Finding the *right* version of this girl, navigating the labyrinthine threads of alternate realities, was a quest that demanded precision, speed, and an unwavering resolve. Time, their most precious commodity, was slipping through their fingers like grains of sand.

He stopped, his reflection staring back at him from a polished section of the wall, the flickering torchlight casting long, dancing shadows that seemed to mock his anxiety. His eyes, normally sharp and filled with an unshakeable confidence, were clouded with doubt. They didn't even have a name, a face, a single defining feature to guide them. They were hunting a ghost, a whisper in the cosmic wind. The sheer magnitude of the challenge was almost paralyzing. How could they possibly hope to locate one specific individual in the vast, teeming expanse of existence? It was like searching for a single, uniquely shaped pebble on an infinite beach. The odds were stacked against them, a mountain of impossibility that threatened to crush their hopes and leave them to the mercy of the encroaching darkness. Yet, Aethon knew, retreat was not an option. The fate of his men, and perhaps the very fabric of reality, rested on their success. They had to find her. They *had* to.

Aethon descended, not merely into the depths of the Bramah stronghold, but into the very heart of existence. He arrived at the roots of the Cosmic Tree, the nexus of all realities, the point from which the multiverse itself unfurled. It was a place of immense power, but also of profound stillness. He lovingly tended to the Tree, offering sustenance as an act of devotion, his fingers tracing the ancient bark. His prayers, whispered into the sacred space, were directed towards two seemingly disparate deities: Althor, the embodiment of protection, guardianship, and justice, and Chronos, the enigmatic god of time, chronology, and the unfolding tapestry of fate. He sought not just their intervention, but their *understanding*, the solace of knowing that the immense burden he carried was witnessed by powers beyond mortal comprehension.

He gazed across the Starseed groves, the leaves shimmering with an ethereal light, stirred by winds that seemed to carry the whispers of creation. The Starseed, the fundamental element revered by the Bramah since the dawn of time, resonated with the very essence of the Cosmic Tree. It represented the enduring, the primordial – a reminder of the continuity that Aethon desperately sought to preserve.

Far across the immeasurable gulf of the multiverse, nestled within the chilling emptiness of the Void, Kael wrestled with his own anxieties. The cryptic explanation he'd received had only deepened his unease. The unsettling possibility of a mortal's involvement felt... insignificant, a discordant note in the symphony of cosmic forces. What role could a fleeting, fragile being possibly play in a conflict that spanned realities? The Blood Rituals, with their attendant descent into near-madness, had left his mind a swirling vortex of chaos. He needed clarity, a still point in the storm.

He ascended to the highest point of the Shivara stronghold, a stark, desolate precipice overlooking the abyss. There, before the Devouring Flame – the Shivara's chilling emblem of consumption and renewal – he sought to center himself. The flickering flames cast dancing shadows, mirroring the turbulent thoughts that raged within him.

I wondered, did Kael's outward demeanor conceal a deeper understanding? He was a master strategist, renowned for his cunning, his ability to mask his true intentions until the opportune moment. His early victories for the Shivara were testament to this calculated secrecy. Aethon, through long and often bitter experience, had learned to anticipate Kael's maneuvers, to a degree. This delicate equilibrium, this hard-won stalemate, had maintained the balance of the multiverse for eons. But the unspoken question lingered: was this balance about to be irrevocably shattered? The introduction of this unknown mortal element hinted at a shift, a potential disruption to the ancient dance between these two cosmic forces, leaving the future hanging precariously in the balance. The very nature of fate, time, and free will were being put to the ultimate test.

A tremor of unease, a cold premonition, snaked through Aethon. Mortals. The very thought of interacting with them again sent a shiver of apprehension down his spine. The consequences were *always* unpredictable, a chaotic cascade of unintended outcomes. New rituals, warped beliefs, entire religions would inevitably sprout in their wake, twisting the truth into something unrecognizable.

The memory of *that* Keystone activation, a cosmic wound that still throbbed with phantom pain, seared his mind. Stars had been born in agony, solar flares had ripped through realities like celestial shrapnel, and countless worlds had been irrevocably changed. That single, cataclysmic event had spawned a thousand new faiths, a tangled web of beliefs that stretched across the multiverse.

He could still feel the heat, the cosmic radiation, the echoes of that ancient crisis. The Shivara, like a creeping, insidious disease, had tightened their grip on a sector of creation. The Dark Gods, their malevolence palpable, were leaking into reality, poisoning world after world. Decay and destruction spread like wildfire, consuming civilizations and leaving behind only ruin and despair. The people, seduced by whispers of darkness, had abandoned the ancient wisdom of the Elder Gods, their gifts of abundance left to fester and rot. A few, the last flickering flames of faith, remained, clinging to their beliefs even as grotesque, nightmare creatures – the twisted creations of the Dark Gods – stalked the land, their fangs dripping with the promise of annihilation. Every good thing, every trace of the Elder Gods' creation, was marked for destruction.

Time was running out. The Bramah, guardians of the cosmic balance, knew they had to act *now*, before the entire quadrant was consumed. A daring, almost reckless plan was hatched – a cosmic surgery to excise the cancerous evil and forge new worlds from the ashes of the old. A crucial world, the linchpin of the entire sector, was teetering on the brink. A colossal solar flare, a wave of cosmic fire, was poised to strike, triggering a planetary deluge, a flood of unimaginable proportions. This was their chance.

Under a veil of secrecy, the Bramah moved, their actions subtle, almost imperceptible. They whispered guidance to righteous men, planting the seeds of salvation – the construction of immense arks, havens of life amidst the coming apocalypse. These were not mere ships; they were vessels of hope, designed to carry the remnants of a dying world towards a fragile new beginning.

But it had to be done *right*. The mortals *must* believe they were acting on divine inspiration, guided by the hand of their Gods, not manipulated by advanced, incomprehensible technology. To reveal their true nature would be to shatter the delicate framework of these nascent societies, a disruption more devastating than even the impending flood. The Bramah became shadows, puppeteers of destiny, guiding the ark builders, orchestrating every detail with meticulous care. As the colossal vessels neared completion, a frantic race against time began, gathering the precious cargo – the seeds of a future that hung precariously in the balance.

Then, the heavens *roared*. The solar flare erupted, a blinding flash of cosmic fury that tore through the atmosphere. The world *convulsed*. The planet itself *shifted* on its axis, a terrifying testament to the raw power unleashed. A monstrous wall of water, a tsunami of unimaginable scale, surged across the land, swallowing everything in its path. Screams, the desperate cries of the doomed, rose above the roar of the deluge, a horrifying chorus that echoed for miles before being brutally silenced by the encroaching waves. The arks, fragile against the cosmic onslaught, were lifted and tossed like toys in a raging storm, their perilous journey just beginning. They were not meant to save *everyone* – only to carry the *possibility* of survival, the flickering flame of hope against the encroaching darkness.

For over a month, these floating islands of life drifted across a drowned world. Inside, families huddled together, their prayers a desperate mantra against the chaos. Unseen, unheard by mortal ears, the Bramah stood vigilant, providing for their needs, while simultaneously engaging in a desperate, hidden war. The Shivara, sensing an opportunity, clawed at the edges of reality, seeking to corrupt this fragile new beginning. The battle raged, a clash of cosmic forces fought in the ethereal realms, unseen by the terrified mortals below. Days bled into nights, a relentless struggle against the encroaching darkness, until finally, with a surge of power, the Bramah repelled the Shivara, casting them back into the suffocating abyss of the Void.

The waters *would* recede. The cosmic storms *would* subside. The arks *would* find their resting place, atop the peaks of what would become majestic mountains, the foundations of a new world. The Bramah *would* then begin their delicate work, weaving the tapestry of life anew, guiding the fledgling civilizations, until the inevitable moment arrived – the moment of departure.

And then? The cycle would begin anew. Myths would arise, legends would be born, whispers of star-travelers and the Gods they served would echo through the generations. Religions, each a unique reflection of that ancient encounter, would bloom and spread, intertwining, merging, evolving. Aethon knew, with a chilling certainty, that it was unavoidable. Every touch, however subtle, left an imprint, a ghostly resonance that would reverberate through time, a constant reminder of the unseen forces that shaped the destiny of worlds. The suspense hung heavy – what new chaos would *this* intervention unleash?

2

Guardians of the Keystones:
Echoes

Chapter Two

Across the gulf of spacetime, across lightyears that stretched the very fabric of reality until it was thin as gossamer, Aethon hurled his consciousness. The great Nexus chamber around him dissolved into a rushing torrent of pure thought as he forged the soul-link with his most trusted commander. It was no mere communication; it was a merging of immortal minds, a connection that defied the cold, unforgiving laws of distance.

On the bridge of the Bramah scout cruiser, *Vigilance*, the stars outside the main viewport blurred into streaks of ethereal light as the soul-link slammed into place. Commander Thorne gripped the arms of his command chair, his knuckles white, his consciousness momentarily straddling two realities—the humming, tense bridge of his ship, and the silent, grand sanctum of his leader.

"Thorne!" Aethon's thought-voice resonated, a burst of raw urgency in the silent void between their minds, sharp and clear above the low thrum of the *Vigilance's* engines. "Report! Has the quarry been sighted? Have you pinpointed the mortal's temporal location?"

Thorne's focus snapped to the immense holographic star-map dominating the center of the bridge, where shimmering webs of probability were being systematically collapsed by his tactical team. "We've collapsed the quantum possibilities, Commander," his response crackled back, tinged with the strain of the relentless search. "Twenty sectors remain within the realm of high probability. We are sweeping the fifth now. The search grid is vast, but we are making progress."

Aethon pressed, the weight of his concern a palpable force across the lightyears. "And the Shivara? Have their shadows fallen across your path?"

Thorne's gaze flickered to a secondary tactical display. On it, their own fleet's icons moved with precision. And mirroring them, always just at the edge of sensor resolution, were faint, ghost-like signatures—Shivara vessels, their drives cloaked, their presence a constant, predatory whisper.

"Affirmative, Commander," Thorne's thought was grim. "They've been dogging our trail since we left the outer territories, a persistent darkness at our heels. They mimic our every move, a pack of Void-hounds waiting for us to show a moment of weakness. My orders? Should we engage in evasive maneuvers?"

"Negative!" Aethon commanded, his thought-voice hardening into tempered steel. "That would only confirm for them that we have a specific target. The mission takes precedence. Do not deviate unless their interference becomes... imminent."

"Understood, sir." A beat of silence, then Thorne's own tightly controlled frustration pierced the soul-link, a rare moment of doubt from the unshakeable commander. "Sir, with all respect... this mortal. The resources we are expending, the risks we are taking, exposing the fleet to Kael's forces... are we certain of her significance? Is she truly the key to restoring the cosmic equilibrium?"

Aethon's reply was not the clear reassurance Thorne sought, but something far more enigmatic, shrouded in the mystery of the vision he'd witnessed. "Her aura, Thorne... when the Gods granted me a glimpse, it radiated something... unique. Not just power, but a harmony so pure it felt like the echo of a song I have long forgotten. A light that, impossibly, casts no shadow. That is all I can discern at this juncture."

The unspoken questions hung heavy in the void between them. Doubt, a dangerous seed, had been sown. Thorne, left with this fragmented, almost poetic reassurance—

"Commander!" a lieutenant shouted from the sensor station, her voice cutting through the bridge's tense quiet. "Massive energy spike! A Shivara vessel decloaking, starboard quarter! They're powering weapon systems!"

Thorne didn't hesitate. "Break the link!" he roared, both aloud and through his connection to Aethon.

The soul-link shattered, the comforting, immense presence of his leader vanishing, leaving Thorne alone on his bridge as alarms blared. He was on his feet, his voice a thunderclap of command. "Evasive maneuvers, full pattern delta! Full power to the shields! Helm, get us behind that gas giant, now!"

The *Vigilance* lurched as it veered sharply, the Shivara ship firing a single, probing lance of dark energy that sizzled past their stern. Then, as quickly as it had appeared, the enemy vessel shimmered and vanished back into the cloak of the Void.

The bridge crew let out a collective, shaky breath. The immediate threat was gone, but the message was clear.

Thorne stood, his jaw tight, staring at the empty space where the Shivara ship had been. They were done testing. They were getting bolder.

"They know we're closing in on something," he said, his voice a low, dangerous growl. "They're trying to force our hand." He turned to his navigator. "Plot a course to the next sector in the probability grid. Maximum speed. The hunt is now a race."

Within the suffocating, infinite blackness of the Shivara stronghold, a storm raged. Kael, a vortex of restless, malevolent energy, stalked the length of his sanctuary. His throne of carved star-metal sat empty behind him, a symbol not of dominion, but of a gnawing, unfulfilled ambition that ate at his very essence. A ravenous fire blazed within him—an ancient, cellular need to finally, decisively, crush the Bramah. To drag them, screaming, from their gilded, orderly worlds and shatter their sanctimonious arrogance on the anvil of true power.

He could envision it: Aethon, Lirien, all of them, in chains of solidified Void, their vaunted light broken, forced to serve the insatiable hunger of the Dark Gods. A curse, ripped from his soul, was spat at the memory of the Elder Gods, those ancient architects of his eternal frustration, the authors of cosmic stagnation. His was not a prayer for guidance; it was a demand for annihilation, for a victory so complete it would burn away the very memory of their Order from the fabric of time.

With a monumental effort of will that made the glyphs on the walls pulse with a violent, crimson light, Kael reined in the tempest. Anger was a tool, not a master. His consciousness, untethered from his physical form, became a phantom, a specter drifting across the vast, shimmering tapestry of the multiverse, narrowing its focus down a single thread of shadow to his Inquisitor. He reached out, his will a piercing arrow, connecting with Vega.

Instantly, the universe resolved into a new perspective. He saw through her eyes, felt the hum of her warship's engines, perceived reality as she did. Thorne's Bramah vessels were ahead, not as mere ships, but as burning scalds of golden, orderly light against the perfect blackness—an offense to the senses. Their energy trails were erratic, chaotic, a frantic search pattern that spoke not of confidence, but of desperation.

"Vega." Kael's voice, a gravelly whisper that bypassed sound and sliced directly into her mind, was sharp with impatience. *"Report. Their movements are frantic. What have you gleaned from their desperation?"*

"They continue their search, my Lord," Vega's mental reply was crisp, clinical, but laced with a subtle undercurrent of a predator's own frustration. *"They are collapsing quantum probabilities across multiple sec-*

tors, *but their pattern is inefficient. It feels... intuitive. As if they follow a ghost, a resonance too faint for our own long-range sensors to isolate. They hunt a specific life-form, but its signature is cloaked, almost non-existent."*

Kael's mental grip tightened, his impatience a tangible force across the link. *"So Aethon throws his best hunters and a full battle group into the dark on a mere premonition? The prize they seek must be of monumental significance."* The silence that followed was thick with barely suppressed fury. The time for subtlety was over. The time for waiting had become an insult.

His command exploded in Vega's mind, a psychic blast of raw, undeniable power. *"Uncover their objective! NOW! I am weary of this chase. Force their hand. Reveal their prize. I want to see what is worth this much effort from Aethon's finest."*

"It will be done, my Lord." Vega's thought was a sharp, perfect blade of obedience.

The soul-link severed. Back on her own bridge, Vega stood, her mind still ringing with the force of her master's command. A cold, terrifying fire now burned in her own eyes, a reflection of Kael's ambition. She turned to her own warriors, silent, shadowy figures who had been waiting, coiled and ready, for this very moment.

A single, unspoken order hung in the air, a promise of brutal, decisive action. *Overtake them. Break them. Rip the secrets from their minds, by any means necessary.*

Her voice was a low, chilling command to her helmsman. "Cloaking protocols rescinded. Power all weapon systems. On my mark, we break their formation."

The hunt had just escalated to a war. The shadows were no longer following; they were closing in for the kill. The air itself vibrated with the promise of imminent violence, of a clash that would determine not just the fate of a mortal girl, but the future of a conflict that could shatter the very foundations of the multiverse.

In a forgotten corner of a parallel reality, lost amongst a swirling sea of universes, a young woman fled through the rain-slicked canyons of neon and neglect. This was Acarcis, the great metropolis on Solara, a city that promised everything and gave nothing. Days of gnawing hunger had finally driven her to the desperate act of theft, and she clutched the meager, stolen scraps—a half-loaf of stale bread—to her chest. It was a victory, a treasure, enough to buy her another sliver of survival. This was her existence, a brutal inheritance from a childhood abandoned to these unforgiving streets. Her name, Eira, was a secret she kept, a faint echo of a life she could barely remember.

She sought refuge in the hollow shell of a derelict municipal building, a place haunted by the ghosts of broken bureaucracy. In a shadowed corner, where the perpetual gloom was thickest, she sank to the floor, her breathing ragged. She began her ritual, a slow, deliberate act of defiance against the gnawing void in her stomach, consuming her stolen sustenance. It was dry, tasteless, but it was life.

Then, a disruption. Distant footsteps, disciplined and steady, echoing in the oppressive quiet. Her hand instinctively sought a weapon—a shard of rusted metal she kept tucked in her boot. This district was a hunting ground after dark, not a sanctuary. The footfalls grew closer, resolving into the indistinct shapes of multiple figures, phantoms of purpose moving through the gloom.

As their muffled, professional voices grew louder, a small, smooth crystal, her only true treasure, found its way from a hidden pocket into her trembling hand. A thought, a breath, a silent prayer breathed into the stone, and the world seemed to shimmer and bend around her. She vanished—or so she believed, her one trick, her only shield. Huddled in her unseen refuge, she listened as they approached, their movements accompanied by the faint, inquisitive hum of strange devices. The leader of the group, his voice a harsh, focused whisper, pointed a scanner directly at her hidden form.

"There," he said, his voice sharp with the thrill of discovery. "The anomaly is localized. Right there!"

A tremor of pure ice ran through her. *They could see her?* Had her veil failed? The crystal had always been her secret, her shield against the horrors of the street.

"We know you're there," the leader's voice cut through the darkness, calm and certain. "Reveal yourself. We mean you no harm. We seek only conversation."

His words were a silken trap. Trust was a luxury Eira could not afford, a currency long since spent. Every promise held a hidden barb, every offer concealed a hook. Yet, they had seen the unseen. Trapped, with escape routes swallowed by their encroaching presence, she reluctantly let her focus drift. Her invisible shield faded like a dying ember. Tears of fear and frustration welled in her eyes, reflecting the dim, uncaring light. Was this the end? Arrested for her petty crime? Or was this something far worse, a fate whispered about in hushed tones—the disappearances, the shadows that snatched people from the streets, never to be seen again?

Hesitantly, her voice barely a breath, she responded, "My name is Eira." It was a surrender, an offering of the only thing she truly possessed.

"Young woman," the leader began, his voice now softer, almost paternal, a tone that sent a fresh wave of fear through her. "I am Dr. Elijah Thompson. I represent an organization known as the Aurora Initiative." He took a slow step closer, his eyes filled with a scientist's profound wonder. "For some time, our instruments have detected... an anomaly. A unique energy signature we could not explain. *You*. We pose no threat. You are, shall we say, of particular and profound interest to us."

Suspicion warred with a desperate, treacherous flicker of hope. Eira extended a trembling hand towards the tall man, her mind a whirlwind of doubt. Was this genuine aid, or just a more meticulously crafted snare? She concealed her crystal, her last vestige of control, deep within a pocket, and allowed herself to be led away. They ushered her from the crumbling decay of her world to a waiting vessel—a star sail, a craft of impossible, silent elegance that ascended into the night, leaving the familiar squalor of Acarcis far, far below.

The short, disorienting flight ended at a monolithic structure that pierced the polluted cityscape. They entered a world utterly alien to Eira. An internal transport, moving with an unnerving, silent speed, carried them deep within the structure's core. Finally, it halted, releasing them into a cavernous laboratory. The sheer scale was overwhelming, a labyrinth where figures in clean, white coats moved with focused intensity, their world one of data and discovery. Eira's body trembled, a fragile leaf in this storm of technological marvel. The opulence, the sheer presence of so many healthy, powerful people, was a shock that stole her breath.

Elijah guided her towards a secluded area dominated by an array of unsettling devices. He gestured towards a chair—an intricate throne of wires and cold, polished metal. "This will not cause you pain," Elijah's voice was a soothing balm that did nothing to quell the rising tide of her fear. "It merely... measures your essence."

Eira approached the contraption with wary reluctance, sinking gingerly into its embrace. Almost immediately, the machinery whirred to life, bathing her in a soft, pulsating light.

"Sir, the readings... they're extraordinary!" a voice exclaimed from a nearby console, laced with a mixture of awe and disbelief. "The anomaly is confirmed. She's... the resonance is perfectly stable! It's beautiful!"

A ripple of excited murmurs spread through the assembled team. Eira shrank further into the chair's confines, a specimen under a microscope, feeling a growing, nameless dread. Elijah placed a hand on her shoulder, a gesture meant to be comforting, but which felt strangely possessive. A smile played on his lips, a smile of pure, triumphant discovery that didn't quite reach his eyes. "Indeed," he murmured, his voice low and heavy with meaning. "You are quite... exceptional." The word hung in the air, laden with an unspoken significance that chilled her to the bone.

Later, a woman with an air of quiet competence introduced herself as Dr. Maya Singh. She escorted Eira to her "accommodations"—a word so foreign it felt like it belonged to another language. The room was a palace to her senses. Simple, clean, uncluttered. She sank into a plush chair, its softness a stark contrast to the hard, unforgiving surfaces of her life. A sense of unreality washed over her. This was... pleasant. Almost unbearably so.

Exhaustion, both physical and emotional, finally claimed her. She drifted towards the large bed, a haven of soft fabric, and succumbed to a sleep filled with uneasy dreams, a precarious blend of hope and apprehension. Even in slumber, the mystery of the Aurora Initiative, and the terrifying question of what made her so interesting, clung to her like a shroud.

The bridge of the Bramah scout cruiser, *Vigilance*, was a vortex of controlled chaos. Data streamed across holographic displays in cascading waterfalls of light, each flicker representing a collapsed probability, a ghost reality discarded in the relentless search for the mortal girl from Aethon's vision.

"Mira, report," Commander Thorne's voice was a low, gravelly rumble that cut through the tension.

"The search grid is focused on the target coordinates from the vision, Commander," his lieutenant replied, her voice crisp, never looking up from her work. "The world designated Solara. I'm attempting to isolate the specific resonance signature now, but the quantum field is unstable."

"Commander!" another officer called out from the sensor station, his voice sharp with alarm. "Shivara shadow signatures are converging on our position! They're not just following anymore—they're running active resonance sweeps on our target sector! Their interference is causing massive signal degradation!"

On Mira's console, the single, pure signature she had been trying to isolate on Solara suddenly fractured, ghosting into a dozen shimmering, unstable echoes. "I'm losing her!" Mira hissed in frustration. "Their interference is scrambling the Acarcis grid. I can't get a solid lock!"

"Lock it down, Mira!" Thorne commanded, his voice cold as the void outside. "Find the prime instance! Now!"

Mira's hands flew across the controls, her expression one of intense concentration. "I'm trying! The core resonance matrix is solid, but the locational data is... shifting! Rerouting through their interference... I have a lock! It's solid! The signature is incredibly strong, almost over-whelming!" she announced, a triumphant energy in her voice. Then, a flicker of confusion. "But... Commander, the coordinates... they're not on Solara."

Thorne was instantly at her side. "What? Report!"

"The target world is... Asphodel," she said, her brow furrowed in dis-belief as she read the impossible data. "And the signature... it's male. And extremely volatile, aggressive even. It must be a reaction to the Shiv-ara scans."

Thorne stared at the screen, his mind racing. Asphodel? A male? It made no sense. The vision was of a girl, in a city. But the Shivara were closing in, their scans undoubtedly getting stronger. "Mira, are you cer-tain the core resonance matches the vision's parameters?"

"Perfectly, sir," she confirmed. "The underlying quantum signature is an identical match. The interference must have... reflected our scan to its twin. Or perhaps this is the true source, and the vision was the echo."

There was no more time for theory. Thorne made the battlefield de-cision. "If the signature matches, he is a key. We cannot let the Shivara find him. Acquire the subject, Mira! Now!"

"Acknowledged, Commander!" Mira's hand slammed down on the transport initiation panel. "Energy spike detected! Locking onto his life signs... isolating him from Asphodel's toxic atmosphere... now!"

In the center of the bridge's transport pad, reality twisted. The air crackled, then tore open with a sickening, silent lurch. A young man materialized—clad in scavenged, mismatched armor, his face smudged with grime, his eyes burning with the feral fury of a cornered predator from a wasteland world. He snarled, already coiling to spring, a lifetime of brutal survival etched into his every muscle.

Before he could launch himself, a med-team was already moving. A single, precise hiss from a soporific agent, and the fight drained from him. The young man's defiant glare slackened, his eyes rolled back, and he collapsed into a heap, succumbing to an induced slumber.

Thorne walked to the transparent wall of the stasis chamber where the subject was being secured. The mission was complete. They had secured the source of the resonance before the Shivara. Yet, a deep, gnawing uncertainty coiled in his gut. This was not the forsaken girl from his commander's vision. This was a hardened survivor from a hell-world. He had made a decision under fire, a choice based on a perfect match to an imperfect signal. He could only pray it was the right one.

He turned back to the bridge, his face an unreadable mask of command. "Helm," he commanded, his voice resonating with grim purpose. "Set a course for the stronghold. Maximum speed. The hunt is over... and the real mystery has just begun."

3

Guardians of the Keystones: Echoes

Chapter Three

Aethon paced the cold, silent expanse of his sanctum, a caged predator in his own revered stronghold. Each passing moment since Thorne's fleet had departed stretched into a torturous eternity. The continued, absolute silence from the Elder Gods was a suffocating weight, now compounded by the operational silence from his most critical mission. The unknown was a poison, and he could bear the agonizing suspense no longer.

Closing his eyes, he focused his immense will, casting the tendrils of his consciousness across the gulf of spacetime. He pierced the veil of distance, forging the soul-link to his general in a single, desperate surge.

"Thorne!" The mental shout was not a request but a blast of raw, undeniable urgency. *"Report!"*

A beat of charged silence, then Thorne's consciousness answered, his mental voice a calm, resonant signal against the backdrop of a distant, humming starship bridge. *"Commander. We are en route back to the stronghold. The operation... was a success. An instance of the designated mortal has been secured."*

A fleeting wave of profound relief washed over Aethon, a brief respite from the gnawing anxiety. But it vanished as quickly as it appeared, replaced by a commander's need for detail. *"The subject's condition? Disposition?"*

There was a subtle hesitation from Thorne, a flicker of something that set Aethon's senses on edge. *"The subject is in stable, induced slumber. As for their disposition... Commander, there are... discrepancies between the vision and the reality."*

Aethon's focus sharpened like a blade. *"Explain."*

"The mortal we have secured is male," Thorne reported, his tone meticulously neutral, yet unable to hide the underlying confusion. *"And the locational lock, once we fought through the Shivara's interference, was not for the world of Solara. It was for the forsaken world of Asphodel. The energy signature was volatile, aggressive... but the core resonance matrix was a perfect, undeniable match to the parameters you provided. The Shivara were closing in. I made a tactical decision to secure the source of the signature."*

A male. From Asphodel. A vessel of rage and volatile energy. Aethon's mind reeled. Everything about it was the antithesis of the vision—the gentle, forsaken girl, the pure, harmonious light. How could this be? How could the Gods show him a beacon of hope, only for the path to lead to this... this hardened survivor from a realm of chaos?

"And the Shivara?" Aethon pressed, a new, cold dread beginning to form. *"What of their interference once you made your move?"*

Thorne's response was what truly chilled him to the core, laced with an unsettling calm that was far more terrifying than a report of battle. *"None, Commander. The moment we initiated transport, their shadow signatures vanished. They simply... let us take him. They remain uncharacteristically quiescent."*

The word hung in the mental space between them, heavy with unspoken dread. *Quiescent.* The Shivara were never quiescent. Their silence was never peace; it was the coiled stillness of a predator waiting for the perfect moment to strike. Past encounters, etched in the bloody annals of their long conflict, screamed that the Shivara should have struck.

They should have fought to claim or destroy the asset. This unnatural stillness... it screamed of a trap.

Aethon's mind raced, trying to decipher the enemy's terrifying strategy. *They drove us to act rashly,* he realized with a sickening certainty. *They scrambled our senses, forced our hand, and then watched as we took the bait.* But for what purpose? What dark design were they weaving? What catastrophic plan lay hidden beneath this unsettling calm?

The question echoed, unanswered, a chilling premonition of a storm yet to break. The silence of the Shivara was not a retreat; it was the terrifying hush before the unleashing of an unimaginable, and perhaps long-planned, chaos.

Eira stirred from a sleep deeper and more profound than any she could remember. It was a slumber born of absolute exhaustion, a final surrender after years of running on fear. Her awakening was heralded not by a harsh noise or a cold reality, but by the quiet, methodical presence of Dr. Maya Singh, who stood nearby, meticulously folding a set of pristine, white garments.

"Ah, you're awake," Dr. Singh's voice was gentle, a stark, unbelievable contrast to the harsh echoes of Acarcis's streets. "You were resting so peacefully, I hesitated to interrupt. It appeared," she paused, her gaze holding a knowing, almost empathetic quality, "that you were in dire need of it."

A faint, uncertain smile played on Dr. Singh's lips. She suggested a cleansing—a shower—and the change of clothes, promising a warm meal would be waiting. Eira, still navigating the bewildering landscape between dream and this new reality, could only nod. This place, this silent, temperature-controlled sanctuary, was a universe removed from the brutal struggle of her former life.

Left alone, she entered the showering chamber. The rush of clean, warm water was a revelation, a luxury so profound it brought tears to her eyes. It washed away not just the grime of the streets, but what felt like layers of ingrained fear and hopelessness. But as the water sluiced away the past, the ever-present question remained, a cold shadow lurking beneath the surface of this impossible opulence: *at what cost?*

The clothes, a soft, dazzling white tunic and trousers, felt alien against skin accustomed to rags. Before dressing, she carefully secreted away her one constant, her one possession of true value—the small, smooth crystal—into a hidden pocket. It was more than a trinket; it was a part of her soul, a secret power she instinctively knew she must conceal from the prying eyes and strange devices of this place.

A soft knock preceded Dr. Singh's return. She guided Eira through long, impersonal corridors of white and brushed metal to a vast, open chamber they called the commissary. With a gesture, Dr. Singh introduced her to the food dispensers, gleaming devices capable of conjuring any imaginable culinary delight. Eira stared, caught between disbelief and a childlike wonder.

"Take only what you require for now, Eira," Maya advised gently, noticing her overwhelmed expression. "These resources will be available to you throughout your... residence here."

The meal was a surreal experience, a feast of flavors that felt like a dream. Afterward, Dr. Singh escorted her back to the main laboratory, where Dr. Elijah Thompson awaited them, an air of keen, scientific anticipation surrounding him. His smile was welcoming, yet held a calculated quality that put Eira on edge.

"While you were recuperating," Dr. Thompson began, his voice smooth and measured, "our systems have been analyzing the unique energy signature we first detected in you, Eira. We have now identified a... resonance. An echo of your signature, originating from a single, distant point in the cosmos." He leaned forward, his eyes alight with intellectual fire. "We wish to investigate this anomaly, to understand its nature and, crucially, its connection to you. Would you be... amenable... to assisting us in this endeavor?"

The question, though phrased as a request, carried the undeniable weight of an expectation. The alternative—a return to the brutal life she knew—was unthinkable. With a hesitant, almost imperceptible nod, she signaled her compliance.

Elijah's smile widened, a flash of pure, triumphant discovery in his eyes. "Excellent," he declared, rising with a decisive movement. "Then let us uncover what awaits us."

The journey into space was a terrifying, beautiful, paradigm-shifting event for Eira. The city, her entire known world, receded below, replaced by the stark, breathtaking velvet of the void, strewn with diamond-dust stars. She had crossed a threshold, leaving everything behind.

Hours later, the bridge was alive with focused energy. "Dr. Thompson, we have confirmation!" Dr. Singh's voice was infused with a quiet excitement. "The signal originates from this planet. Definitive localization achieved."

"Prepare a landing party," Elijah commanded, his voice resonating with purpose. "We disembark immediately."

The team descended onto the surface of an unknown world, a small cluster of figures dwarfed by the immensity of the alien landscape. A short distance away, nestled within a breathtaking valley between towering, silent mountain sentinels, lay an ancient city—a ghost of civilization, seemingly untouched by the passage of time. And perched precariously on one of the mountain peaks, a colossal citadel dominated the skyline.

A flicker of impossible recognition sparked within her, a name surfacing from the depths of a past she could not identify. *Elyria.*

They proceeded with wary caution along a timeworn road toward a central shrine, their instruments registering an increasingly potent energy signature. Within the shrine's shadowed interior, the source intensified. A hidden spiral staircase, descending into the earth, beckoned them downwards into the labyrinthine depths of the catacombs. Deeper and deeper they ventured, until the passage opened into a vast, subterranean chamber.

There, bathed in an ethereal, almost unearthly glow, was a massive altar. And above it, suspended in the air as if defying gravity, pulsed a crystal of impossible size, its facets catching the strange light, its core seeming to hold a slow, silent, living heartbeat.

The very air crackled with unseen energy. Eira felt a sympathetic resonance within her own hidden crystal, a powerful warmth that bordered on burning, a vibration that hummed through her very being. A secret knowledge stirred within her, a terrifying and exhilarating premonition, yet she remained silent, guarding her treasure.

"Any discernible inscriptions?" Elijah's voice, though controlled, betrayed a hint of profound awe. "Anything that might shed light on the nature of this... artifact?"

"There are markings, sir," Dr. Singh replied, her voice hushed. "On the far wall. Ancient... possibly a form of proto-language."

"Decipher them," Elijah ordered, his gaze fixed on the pulsating crystal, his scientific curiosity warring with a primal sense of fear. "And swiftly. We are in a realm of unknown variables."

He didn't need to articulate the unspoken dread that settled over them all. They were intruders in a sacred space, tampering with forces they barely understood, and the consequences of their actions were utterly, terrifyingly, unpredictable.

The proximity alarm shrieked—a soul-shredding klaxon that ripped through the tense, operational silence of the *Vigilance*'s bridge. On the main tactical display, a single, hostile signature materialized from the Void, shedding its cloak with the sudden, violent grace of a predator revealing its fangs. The Shivara. They were closing fast.

"Battle stations!" Thorne's roar was a thunderclap, a shockwave of pure command that galvanized the Bramah warriors into immediate, disciplined action. Consoles flared to life, shields hummed with immense, rising power, and weapons systems came online with a low, deadly thrum.

An instant later, Vega's battlecruiser, a sleek, menacing blade of obsidian and malevolent light, filled the main viewscreen, bearing down on them with undeniable lethal intent. The silent prayer Thorne had harbored for a clean, bloodless extraction shattered into a million pieces. This confrontation could no longer be avoided.

Energy blasts, lances of corrosive purple energy, ripped across the void, impacting their shields with bone-jarring, deafening force. The entire ship screamed under the assault, a groaning protest of tortured metal, and the air grew thick with the scent of ozone and the sharp, acrid smell of burning circuitry.

Vega's face, a perfect mask of cruel, arrogant amusement, flickered onto the viewscreen. Her voice was a venomous whisper designed to unnerve and demoralize. "Thorne," she purred, the sound dripping with condescension. "Always so predictable. Why prolong the inevitable? Spare your crew the agony. Surrender your precious, mysterious cargo, and perhaps I will grant you the mercy of a swift death. You know my power eclipses that of your pathetic transport."

"The battle has barely begun, Vega," Thorne retorted, his voice a granite-hard counterpoint to her taunting, his hands gripping his command chair. "You've always favored the coward's path, lurking in shadows, striking from ambush. A true warrior faces their opponent head-on!"

"My skills are superior in every conceivable way, Thorne," Vega hissed, her eyes glittering with a chilling malice. "This is not a battle; it is a culling. Relinquish your prize now, or I will tear your ship apart piece by piece and take it from your cooling corpse."

"Never, Vega!" Thorne's defiance was absolute, a roar of conviction. "Return to the abyss you crawled from! Bramah space is forbidden to you and your dark masters!"

A cruel, slow smirk twisted Vega's lips as her image flickered and vanished. She turned her full, terrifying attention to the attack, unleashing a relentless, overwhelming barrage of energy fire. But Thorne, a veteran of countless impossible battles, was a master of strategy. He weaved his ship through the deadly, incandescent onslaught with breathtaking skill, each maneuver a desperate, calculated gamble. With every evasive action, he edged them closer, ever closer, to the Bramah stronghold—a distant beacon of hope in the gathering storm. Desperate, he reached out, his mind a focused tendril of urgent need, forging the soul-link with Aethon. The plea for reinforcements was a silent scream across the vastness of space. Aethon's response was immediate—a surge of reassurance and the promise of imminent aid.

But time was running out. Thorne's ship, battered and groaning, was nearing its breaking point. Shields were failing, hull breaches spiderwebbing across the lower decks. He was a wounded lion, cornered and defiant, but he could not hold out indefinitely.

A final, shuddering impact ripped through the *Vigilance*, a groaning protest of metal pushed beyond its limits. Thorne braced himself, knowing the next hit might be the last. Just as despair threatened to engulf him, five blazing comets of golden light erupted from folded space—Bramah warships, their arrival a sudden, vengeful constellation. They materialized with pinpoint precision, forming a protective cordon around Thorne's crippled ship, a steel gauntlet thrown in the face of Vega's aggression.

On the bridge of her battlecruiser, Vega's face contorted in a mask of disbelief and pure fury. Her carefully orchestrated ambush had been shattered, her prey snatched from her grasp. The Bramah, no longer constrained by defense, unleashed a devastating, coordinated barrage. Searing lances of pure, destructive energy slammed into her vessel.

Shields flared, buckled, and collapsed under the overwhelming, concentrated onslaught.

The hunter had become the hunted. For a split second, a flicker of raw panic crossed Vega's face, quickly replaced by a snarl of frustrated rage. Survival was the only imperative. With a burst of blinding speed, she engaged her slip drive, tearing a violent, ragged hole in the fabric of space-time and vanishing in a distorted shimmer of light—a wounded beast fleeing a battle it could no longer win.

With Vega's forces routed, the Bramah warships shifted their focus, turning their immense power towards Thorne's ravaged vessel. A visible stream of energy enveloped the stricken ship like a healing embrace. As one, the reunited fleet turned, aligning themselves towards the distant stronghold and vanishing into folded space, reappearing moments later in the protective orbit of their home base.

Aethon, watching from the command center, felt a wave of profound but hollow relief. His forces were safe, the immediate threat averted. But the knowledge Thorne had imparted through the soul-link—the impossible truth of their quarry—was a cold, heavy weight in his mind.

Thorne, his face etched with the weariness of battle and a deep, underlying uncertainty, approached the command dais. The two leaders clasped arms, a silent acknowledgment of the peril survived and the mystery that now confronted them.

"Your success under fire was remarkable, my friend," Aethon said, his voice low and grave, his eyes searching Thorne's for answers. "But confirm it for me, face-to-face. What you reported... it is true? The subject you hold is a male from Asphodel."

"Yes, Commander," Thorne affirmed, his voice steady but tense. "As I reported. The Shivara interference was overwhelming, scrambling all locational data tied to the vision's origin point on Solara. But the core quantum resonance—the very signature the Gods revealed to you—flared on Asphodel. It was a perfect match. In the moment, with the enemy closing in, I chose to trust the signature above all else. It was the only tactical option."

Aethon nodded slowly, his gaze distant. He understood the battlefield logic, but it did not solve the divine riddle. "A perfect match to the energy... and a perfect contradiction to the vision." He began to pace, the weight of the paradox settling on him. "The Gods showed me a gentle girl, a beacon of pure, harmonious light in a city of shadows. And you bring me a hardened survivor, a boy forged in the fires of a forsaken world like Asphodel. It cannot be both a coincidence and a perfect match. This feels... like a trap. A question I do not know how to answer."

His gaze hardened with resolve. "If theology presents a paradox, perhaps science can offer a variable. I must see Lila's analysis."

Aethon strode towards the science labs, his mind a storm of conflict. He found Lila overseeing the transfer of the slumbering mortal into a high-level containment and analysis field. She looked up as he entered, her expression one of profound, scientific disbelief.

"Lila. Report," Aethon commanded, his voice tight. "Tell me what you have found. What is the nature of a being that can carry the pure, harmonious resonance from my vision, yet be its complete physical antithesis?"

Lila, her gaze still fixed on the perplexing data streaming across her monitors, shook her head slowly. "Commander... it defies all logic. The readings are confirmed and reconfirmed—it is the precise frequency we sought, the exact signature. But for a mortal, any mortal, to be a natural conduit for this level of Keystone energy... it's beyond our comprehension. It shouldn't be possible." She paused, her brow furrowed. "And for that energy to be housed in a subject from a world as chaotic and Void-tainted as Asphodel... Aethon, the two concepts are mutually exclusive. It is like finding a perfect, living star burning in the heart of a black hole."

Aethon's voice was a strained whisper, his faith and his strategic mind clashing in a silent, internal war. "My vision... it showed me a young woman, with unmistakable clarity. The Gods are never ambiguous. This... this throws everything into disarray." He looked at the unconscious form of the boy, this impossible contradiction. "I must seek further counsel. This paradox must be illuminated."

Driven by a desperate need for answers, Aethon turned and made his way towards the Cosmic Tree—a sacred nexus within the stronghold where the veil between the immortal realm and the divine was at its thinnest. There, amidst the ethereal glow of the ancient, silent tree, he hoped to re-establish the broken connection, to find clarity in the face of this bewildering contradiction, to understand why the Gods' vision and the universe's reality had diverged so drastically.

4

Guardians of the Keystones:
Echoes

Chapter Four

In the heart of the Bramah stronghold, where the roots of the celestial Cosmic Tree intertwined with glowing veins of pure energy, Aethon knelt in silent, desperate supplication. This sacred chamber, usually alive with the gentle, rustling whispers of the divine flowing through the Tree's shimmering, starlit leaves, was now utterly, unnervingly still. For days, he had sought counsel at this living nexus, a conduit to his creators, only to be met with a profound and hollow silence that echoed the doubt in his own immortal heart.

Just as the weight of that silence became unbearable, a change began.

A single leaf on the highest bough of the Cosmic Tree began to glow with a soft, silver luminescence. The light dripped down the ancient bark like liquid starlight, pooling at the Tree's base and coalescing into a serene, radiant form. From this gentle nexus of light, the divine emissary Nyx emerged, her presence a balm of profound peace in the troubled chamber.

Her voice was like the chime of distant, sacred bells, speaking not just to his ear, but to his soul. "Aethon, First of the Bramah. Your vigil is ended. Your plea has been heard."

Aethon, who had remained steadfast, rose from his kneeling position, his face a mask of profound relief and reverence. "Radiant Nyx. Forgive my doubt. The silence... it has been a trial for us all."

"A great disturbance shook the foundations of reality, noble Aethon," Nyx's voice soothed. "The Divine Ones turned their full will to mending the fraying threads of creation. You were not abandoned. Now, their gaze turns outward, and they send you a message. A vision. A purpose."

She raised a luminous hand, and Aethon felt her presence touch his mind. The chamber of the Cosmic Tree dissolved, replaced by a vision of a place both alien and sterile. He saw the mortal girl from his first vision, her inner light still a brilliant, defiant spark. But she was not huddled in a rain-slicked alley, forsaken and alone.

She was in a cage of clean, white walls and gleaming metal, observed by other mortals who moved with a quiet, unnerving authority. She was dressed in pristine white, a specimen, not a beggar. He saw them guide her, their instruments probing the pure, harmonious resonance that was her essence. These were not ignorant creatures; they were intelligent, organized, and powerful in their own right, their command of technology a force to be reckoned with. They were studying a power they did not comprehend, like curious children playing with a star.

The vision faded, leaving Aethon with a new, more complicated sense of dread.

"The spark we have revealed to you is not lost in the wilderness, Aethon," Nyx's voice was now imbued with a solemn gravity. "It is already held within a cage of keen mortal artifice."

Her directive was absolute, a sacred command layered with caution. "You must retrieve this girl. She is an echo of Creation's dawn, a key to the dissonance that now threatens the balance. But you must tread with great care. The mortals who hold her are not the brutish forces of Chaos. They are a significant power in their own realm. A direct assault could shatter the very thing you seek to save, or ignite a new war that the multiverse cannot afford. Prudence and wisdom must be your primary weapons in this endeavor."

The weight of uncertainty that had plagued Aethon was lifted, only to be replaced by the immense burden of a far more delicate and perilous mission. He was no longer a general planning a rescue, but a diplomat planning an incursion.

"I understand, Radiant One," he vowed, his voice resonating with a new, focused resolve. "We will proceed with the utmost care. The girl will be brought into our protection."

A gentle, approving smile touched Nyx's ethereal features. "Their light guides your path, Aethon, even when it is veiled by mortal ambition."

With a final, benedictory nod, her form dissolved, receding back into the great Tree, its silver light fading from the leaves. Aethon stood alone, but no longer adrift. His path was clear, though fraught with dangers he had not anticipated. His holy quest had begun not with a simple act of salvation, but with the complex challenge of navigating a powerful and unknown mortal faction that now held a key to the fate of the cosmos.

The subterranean chamber hummed with a power that vibrated in the teeth. It was a low, pervasive thrum that seemed to emanate not just from the colossal, pulsing crystal, but from the very stones of the ancient shrine. Dr. Elijah Thompson paced anxiously, a predator in his own cage of discovery, his eyes flicking between the chaotic, beautiful data streaming onto his team's equipment and the impossible artifact itself. The readings were a scientist's dream and a logician's nightmare—patterns that defied known physics, energy signatures that hinted at other dimensions.

But another sound wormed its way into his awareness: a soft, rhythmic whimpering. He turned, his focus finally breaking from the data. In the back of the chamber, half-hidden by the glow of a sensor array, was Eira. She was curled into a tight ball on the cold floor, rocking back and forth, her hands pressed hard against her temples. Her face was ashen, beaded with a cold sweat of profound distress.

"Eira?" He approached her cautiously, his voice softer than he intended, laced with a genuine, startled concern. "What is it? What's wrong?"

Her response was a strained, fractured whisper, barely audible above the chamber's oppressive hum. "The humming... It's not like before. It's... wrong." She squeezed her eyes shut. "It's hurting my head. It feels... angry. And sad. Like a scream and a sob all at once. I don't think I can stand it much longer."

Elijah frowned, his scientific curiosity momentarily overshadowed by a physician's concern. But her words—*angry and sad*—were data points, too. "We're almost done here," he said, offering a reassuring smile that felt thin and inadequate. "We can leave soon, you'll be able to rest. Just try to hold on. What we're learning here is vital. We're on the verge of understanding what this thing truly is." He knew he was asking the impossible, but the data was too precious. He was also acutely aware of the time, of the immense energy their activities were broadcasting across systems. They were a beacon, and he did not know what might answer the call.

"Okay," he said decisively, turning back to his team. "Let's prepare for extraction. We're taking the crystal back to the lab. We can study it more safely there."

Dr. Singh looked up from her console, her own expression deeply troubled. "Sir," she said, her voice hushed with a mixture of awe and terror. "We've tried. Our gravimetric sensors can't get a lock. The readings are... impossible. Its mass is variable, fluctuating between something manageable and a value approaching infinity. We can't move it because it's not just floating here. It's... anchored. To something that isn't in this dimension."

Elijah stared at the crystal, his confidence beginning to fray at the edges, replaced by a creeping, primal dread. "How is that even possible?"

"I honestly don't know, sir," Maya admitted. "It's violating several fundamental laws of physics simultaneously."

He paused, the hum of the chamber seeming to grow louder, more menacing. He weighed their options, the risk of staying against the value of the prize. "Do we have enough data for now? Can we analyze what we have?"

"Yes, sir," Dr. Singh confirmed, her relief palpable. "It will take our best systems weeks, perhaps months, to fully process everything we've already collected."

"Alright," Elijah said, his voice sharp with a finality that broke the spell of scientific wonder. "Pack it up. We're leaving. Now. This place... it doesn't feel safe anymore."

A new urgency seized the team. The excitement of discovery was replaced by the tense efficiency of a strategic retreat. They began to dismantle their equipment, their movements swift, eager to escape the chamber's oppressive atmosphere.

Eira continued to rock, the humming a constant, unsettling presence in her mind. But now, she could feel it more clearly. It *was* two distinct feelings, two warring resonances wrapped around each other, emanating from the great crystal and vibrating within her own hidden shard. One was a profound, heartbreaking sorrow—a lament she understood on a deep, instinctual level. The other was a raw, seething rage, an alien feeling that terrified her, a violent energy that was utterly foreign to her own nature. The mystery of the great crystal had been replaced by a more intimate and terrifying one: why did this impossible, warring consciousness feel like a part of her own?

Aethon, his voice laced with urgency, summoned Thorne to the command center. Thorne arrived promptly, sensing the shift in Aethon's demeanor – a clear indication of significant developments.

"Sir," Thorne inquired, "did your communion with the Gods provide clarity? Regarding the female mortal?"

"Yes," Aethon confirmed, his voice carrying a weight of newfound purpose. "Her existence is confirmed. And our imperative is clear: we *must* locate her. Immediately."

Thorne's expression reflected a mixture of concern and professional assessment. "Sir, with all due respect, the search parameters remain vast. Identifying her could require a considerable expenditure of resources and time..."

Aethon interrupted, a spark of determined hope in his eyes. "Perhaps... the male subject we secured possesses information. Knowledge that could narrow our search. Awaken him. We require an interrogation."

"As you command, sir." Thorne departed, leaving Aethon to gaze out at the breathtaking panorama of the cosmos – a swirling canvas of stars and nebulae, a visual representation of the immense task before them.

Thorne contacted Aethon, requesting his presence in the laboratory holding the mortal subject. The young man, now conscious, was seated on an examination table, his posture radiating a mixture of defiance and simmering anger. Lila was attempting to continue her analysis, but the subject's lack of cooperation was hindering her efforts. Aethon approached, his presence radiating authority, and grasped the young man's arm with firm, but not brutal, force.

"State your name," Aethon requested, his voice firm yet controlled.

"Erebus," the young man retorted, the name delivered with a defiant edge. "And I demand to know who *you* are, and by what right you have abducted me!"

"Erebus," Aethon repeated, his voice moderating slightly, attempting a more measured approach. "Please, try to remain calm. We harbor no hostile intentions. You possess a unique quality. A resonance... an energy signature that aligns with a... sacred artifact of immense importance. A Keystone. A crystal imbued with great power. Are you aware of this connection?"

Erebus's defiance wavered at the mention of "crystal." A flicker of fear, of guarded knowledge, passed across his face. He had believed his secret was secure. The technology surrounding him, though utterly foreign, hummed with a power that felt both advanced and strangely... ancient. His studies, extensive as they were, had never hinted at anything like this. It seemed almost magical.

He hesitated, then, his voice tinged with suspicion, he inquired, "I *may* have some knowledge of such an object. What is your objective? Are you attempting to... purchase it? Steal it? Sell it? What possible need could beings of your apparent stature have for material wealth or conventional power?"

"It is an object of profound spiritual significance," Aethon explained, his tone taking on a note of reverence. "Created by the beings we revere as Gods. It is vital to our order. Is this crystal... intrinsically linked to you, or merely an item in your possession?"

Reluctantly, almost fearfully, Erebus unclenched his fist, revealing a small, luminescent crystal resting in his palm. He offered it, with visible apprehension, to Lila. Aethon observed the exchange with intense fascination. It was a *fragment*, a sliver broken from a Keystone – a concept he had considered theoretically impossible.

Lila, receiving the shard with the utmost care, immediately initiated a series of diagnostic scans. The laboratory hummed with the activity of her instruments. Finally, she straightened, her expression a mixture of profound astonishment and scholarly excitement. She addressed Aethon, her voice hushed with awe.

"It's... inextricably linked to him, sir. On a fundamental, energetic level. The Keystone's power... it flows *through* him. I have never encountered anything remotely similar in all my years of research."

Aethon's gaze shifted from Lila back to the crystal fragment, then to Erebus himself, his mind grappling with the extraordinary implications. "The specific origin of this fragment...can you determine which Keystone it is derived from?"

Lila nodded, her voice still carrying that note of barely suppressed wonder. "Yes. With certainty. This fragment...originates from the *Prime* Keystone." The pronouncement hung in the air, heavy with significance, a revelation that resonated with the force of a cosmic revelation. The mystery had taken on a new, even more daunting dimension, and the path forward, though illuminated by this new knowledge, was fraught with unforeseen challenges.

Aethon's mind raced, grappling with the implications of this astonishing revelation. The *Prime* Keystone. Was its fragmentation somehow linked to the multiversal disruption? The very notion was staggering, the possibilities both terrifying and exhilarating. He forced himself to focus, pushing aside the cosmic implications for the moment, and returned his attention to Erebus.

"Erebus," Aethon began, his voice carefully measured, "are you aware of a young woman, a female, who might possess abilities similar to your own, connected to this... resonance?"

Erebus paused, his brow furrowed in concentration. "No... but... wait. Yes. There *is* a presence. Faint. In my dreams, sometimes. I sense... fear. She's in a place... she doesn't know if she can trust it."

Aethon leaned forward, his interest intensely focused. "Can you identify her location? Anything specific?"

Erebus closed his eyes, seemingly straining to grasp a fleeting image. "A world... Solara. A city... Acarcis. She's... being held. By a group... the Aurora Initiative. Her name... is Eira."

"Exceptional, Erebus," Aethon said, a sense of profound relief and renewed urgency washing over him. "Your cooperation has been invaluable. We would be grateful if you would remain with us, for a time. We have much to accomplish, and your assistance could prove crucial."

"Yes, sir," Erebus replied, a hint of resignation in his voice.

Aethon turned, summoning Thorne with a gesture. They retreated to the command center, the weight of their new knowledge pressing upon them. Aethon, struggling to anticipate the Shivara's next move, found himself wrestling with a multitude of uncertainties. Would they renew their attack? Were they lying in wait, anticipating the Bramah's next action? He stilled his racing thoughts, focusing on the immediate task. Placing a hand on Thorne's shoulder, a gesture of both trust and shared burden, he spoke.

"We must retrieve this girl, Eira, swiftly and discreetly. But we know nothing of this 'Aurora Initiative'. Their motives, their capabilities... are unknown."

"Perhaps... a diplomatic approach, sir?" Thorne suggested. "A negotiation, a mutually beneficial agreement?"

Aethon nodded slowly, considering the possibility. "It is a path we must explore. But," his voice hardened, "whatever course we choose, we must act decisively, without hesitation. Thorne, you will lead this mission. Secure the girl. Bring her here. By any means necessary."

"Understood, sir."

"And this time," Aethon added, a grim determination in his eyes, "you will not travel alone. I am assigning three battleships to your command. I anticipate... complications."

"Thank you, sir."

Thorne, wasting no time, assembled his team and departed, this time leading a formidable force, prepared for whatever challenges lay ahead. The quest for the girl, Eira, had begun – a race against time, against unknown enemies, and against the looming shadow of a cosmic mystery that threatened to unravel the fabric of reality.

Thorne monitored his team as they worked hurriedly to find their target, this unique mortal that held the hope of the future in their hands. He thought back on his own journey that brought him into the service of the Bramah and the Elder Gods. It was so long ago, in a place so different from the life he knows today.

Before he was Thorne of the Bramah, a name forged in divine fire and immortal sorrow, he was Tarek of the Stone Guard. His home was Khyber, a harsh world perpetually locked in twilight, its weakened sun a distant, hazy smudge behind dense, swirling nebulae. It was a world of scarcity and hardship, breeding a people who were resilient, pragmatic, and fiercely loyal to their own. They were survivors, organized into fortified city-states that constantly vied for resources and defended themselves from the predatory fauna that stalked the gloaming lands.

It was in this unforgiving forge that Tarek was made. He lived in the city-state of Athelburg, rising through the ranks of its defense force not from noble birth, but by sheer will, unwavering courage, and an innate ability to lead his people through the most desperate situations. By the time the Shivara came, he was a seasoned Commander, respected for his calm under fire. He bore the scars of countless skirmishes, but his strength came not just from the battlefield, but from the life he fought to protect: his wife, Lyra, whose strength was his anchor, and his young daughter, a child whose laughter was the only true light on their twilight world.

Four hundred years ago, the sky over Khyber tore open. The Shivara laid siege to Athelburg, not for its meager resources, but for the hidden nexus of ley lines that converged beneath it—a cosmic anchor they could corrupt to destabilize the entire sector. Their arrival, led by a powerful Sorcerer-Lord, was brutal and overwhelming.

The Bramah, led by Aethon himself, detected the plan and moved to intervene, but they arrived mid-battle. Athelburg's outer defenses had crumbled, and the Shivara were making their final, bloody push into the heart of the city.

Tarek and his remaining Stone Guard were the last line of defense, holding a narrow, crumbling causeway against waves of chittering Shivara shock troops. It was then that Tarek witnessed the miracle of the

Bramah, beings of pure light and power descending into the battle like avenging angels. But they were engaged with the bulk of the Shivara forces, unable to reach the Sorcerer-Lord in time as he began a devastating ritual to shatter the final gateway.

In that moment of absolute clarity, Tarek made a choice. A final image flashed in his mind: Lyra's face, strong and loving; his daughter's small hand clutching his finger. He didn't know if they had made it to the inner shelters. He might never know. But he knew he could give them a chance.

Ordering his few remaining soldiers to hold the line to their last breath, he seized the Guard's most sacred, volatile artifact: a containment device holding unstable rift energy, a last-resort city defense bomb.

He charged. Alone.

He fought through the Sorcerer-Lord's personal guard, a berserker fury driving him on. Blades tore at his armor and flesh, but he ignored the grievous wounds, his entire being focused on a single, final act of defiance. He broke through the final line and, with the last of his strength, detonated the device at the feet of the horrified Sorcerer-Lord. The resulting explosion was not just fire, but a silent, violent un-making of reality that vaporized the Sorcerer-Lord and his servants, disrupting the dark ritual and creating the opening the Bramah needed to finally crush the remaining Shivara forces. Tarek, caught at the epicenter of the blast, was shattered.

As his life faded on the scorched causeway, his spirit blazed with a love for his family and a selfless duty to his city. The Elder Gods, observing through the eyes of the Bramah, were moved. They saw a mortal embodying the very principles of balance and protection they championed.

They intervened. They pulled his spirit back from the brink of oblivion and offered him a choice: peace in the afterlife, or continued service on a grander, cosmic scale. Filled with the burning desire to prevent other worlds from suffering Khyber's fate, knowing he could never return to the life that was, to the family he may have already lost, he accepted.

The Elder Gods reforged his body, granting him immortality. They bestowed upon him the name **Thorne**, symbolizing his resilience and the pain he had endured. He was inducted into the Command Guard, the only mortal ever granted such an honor. His new life was a trial. The question of whether his wife and daughter had survived the siege haunted his quiet moments, a wound that even immortality could not heal. He could never go back. To them, he was a ghost, a martyr. To him, they were a sacred memory, a source of unending, silent grief.

But Thorne proved himself through centuries of unwavering service. His tactical brilliance, honed on Khyber, and his firsthand understanding of mortal fear and courage made him one of Aethon's most trusted commanders, his personal sorrow forged into an unshakeable resolve to protect the innocent across the multiverse.

As the vessel docked, merging seamlessly with the Aurora Initiative headquarters, Eira was still deeply disturbed by the strange behavior of her crystal. The *humming*, the unusual warmth – it defied all logic and reason. Never, in all the years she had possessed it, had it manifested such characteristics. Lost in this perplexing contemplation, a new sensation pierced her awareness – a *presence*, a feeling of being observed, yet she was demonstrably alone.

Then, a voice. Clear, resonant, yet undeniably *inside* her mind, a violation of her innermost self. *"Eira. Can you hear me?"* It was not her own internal voice, not a thought, but an intrusion, both alien and strangely familiar.

A wave of disorientation, of profound unreality, washed over her. *"Eira, can you hear me?"* The voice persisted, patient, yet insistent.

"Who... who are you?" Eira's response was a mental whisper, a hesitant foray into the unknown.

"I am Erebus. I perceived your presence... within my own mind. And... something else. A vastness... I don't understand it. Do you?"

"No," Eira responded, her mental voice gaining a fraction of strength. *"I feel it too. This connection... how is it possible?"*

"I do not know," Erebus admitted. *"You possess a crystal fragment, do you not?"*

"Yes," Eira confirmed, a growing sense of wonder mingling with her apprehension. *"And you?"*

"I do," Erebus replied. *"I believe... these fragments... they are a conduit, a bridge between us."*

"The large crystal," Eira ventured, the image of the pulsating Keystone vivid in her mind. *"Could it be related? To our connection?"*

"Undoubtedly," Erebus responded, his mental voice tinged with awe and a growing unease. *"I could perceive it, through your senses. Feel your reaction. It possesses a... sentience... of a kind. But its nature... it remains obscured."*

"It felt... angry," Eira confessed, the memory of that unsettling emotion still vivid. *"But how can a crystal feel? It defies reason."*

"Reason may not be sufficient to comprehend this," Erebus replied. Then, a sudden urgency, a sharp edge of warning, entered his mental voice. *"Eira. I must impart something of grave importance. You are in peril. Imminent peril. You will sense the moment. When it arrives... flee!"*

"What? Peril? From whom?" Eira's mind reeled, the sense of disorientation intensifying.

"I cannot fully comprehend it," Erebus admitted, *"Only... a premonition. A certainty. Remember. Flee!"*

The intrusion of reality shattered the ethereal connection. Dr. Singh entered, her presence a jarring return to the physical world. Eira instinctively, almost frantically, concealed the crystal once more, burying it deep within her pocket. The words of Erebus echoed in her mind, a chilling prophecy. *Danger.* But from what? From whom?

"Are you prepared, Eira?" Dr. Singh inquired, her voice betraying no hint of the extraordinary conversation that had just transpired. "We have arrived."

"Yes," Eira managed, her voice barely a whisper.

Dr. Singh paused, her gaze scrutinizing Eira's face. "You appear... perturbed. Is something amiss?"

"No," Eira lied, forcing a semblance of calm. *"Merely... tired."*

"Rest will be provided soon," Dr. Singh assured her, her tone soothing, yet somehow failing to reassure. "Come. Let us proceed." The mystery of the crystal, the connection with Erebus, the warning of imminent danger – all these threads wove a tapestry of increasing complexity and unease, leaving Eira suspended between a fragile hope and a growing, profound sense of dread. The future had become a swirling vortex of uncertainty, and she was caught in its inexorable pull.

The last of Elijah's team, their movements hurried in the unsettling silence of the docking bay, were unloading the vessel's enigmatic cargo. Elijah, flanked by Dr. Singh, escorted Eira – a captive or a guest, she could not be sure – across the threshold, into the heart of the Aurora Initiative. As the final member of the team, a man named Caleb Reyes, stepped onto the platform, a phenomenon of impossible darkness manifested behind him. It was not mere shadow, but an absence of light itself, a *void* that coalesced into a swirling, black mist.

Within this inky miasma, a portal – or perhaps a *tear* in the fabric of reality – ripped open. It was not a doorway to a place, but to an *unplace*, a realm of absolute nothingness that defied comprehension. From the heart of this impossible gateway, two hands, gnarled and scarred, like the claws of some ancient, predatory beast, reached out with terrifying speed. They seized Caleb Reyes, their grip inescapable, and before a scream could even form in his throat, he was yanked violently into the black abyss. The portal, the mist, the man – all vanished in an instant, leaving behind only a chilling void where they had been.

But from that void, something *else* emerged. Tendrils of pure darkness, like living shadows, snaked out from the point where the portal had been, slithering across the floor with unnatural speed, their focus, with terrifying certainty, fixed on Eira. A wave of primal terror, a cold dread unlike anything she had ever experienced, washed over her. And within the echoing chambers of her mind, the warning of Erebus, a desperate cry across the impossible gulf between them, screamed: *Run!* The world had tilted on its axis, plunging from a realm of unsettling mystery into one of pure, unadulterated nightmare.

Eira fled, propelled by a primal instinct, her lungs burning, her heart hammering against her ribs. She plunged into the relative sanctuary of the Aurora Initiative headquarters, a desperate flight from an unimaginable horror. Dr. Singh and Elijah, startled by her sudden, frantic arrival, whirled around to witness the last wisps of the unnatural black mist dissipating into nothingness, leaving behind only the chilling absence of Caleb Reyes. Elijah's voice, sharp and commanding, cut through the stunned silence, ordering an immediate security lockdown, a futile attempt to contain a threat that had already come and gone.

Dr. Singh, her face etched with concern, hurried towards Eira, her voice a soothing counterpoint to the rising panic. "Eira, are you unharmed?"

"Yes," Eira gasped, the word a shaky exhalation. "I... I *felt* it. A warning... in my mind."

"It's over now," Dr. Singh said, her words meant to reassure, but carrying a hollow ring in the face of the inexplicable events. "You're safe." She gently guided Eira back towards the relative seclusion of her quarters, urging her to rest. The unspoken truth hung heavy between them: the work ahead was fraught with unknown dangers, and Eira's well-being was paramount. Guards, their faces grim and alert, were posted outside Eira's door, a fragile barrier against the encroaching darkness.

Left behind in the now eerily silent docking bay, Elijah, his expression a mask of grim determination, surveyed the scene of the abduction. He directed a team of technicians, their instruments humming with a faint, almost pathetic inadequacy, to scan the area, searching for any lingering trace, any residual energy signature that might offer a clue to the nature of the portal and the fate of Caleb Reyes. The data was crucial, but it was the rescue of his colleague, the unraveling of this terrifying mystery, that consumed his thoughts.

Far below the gleaming towers of the city, deep within a hidden cavern, a crude shrine pulsed with a malevolent energy. Here, amidst shadows and the chilling whispers of forgotten rituals, the Order of the Veil, a cult steeped in darkness and devoted to the terrifying power of the Dark Gods and their Shivara emissaries, held sway. The abduction of Caleb Reyes was but the first move in a game of cosmic proportions, a game where the stakes were nothing less than the fate of reality itself. The veil between worlds had thinned, and the shadows were stirring.

Guardians of the Keystones: Echoes

Chapter Five

Caleb's consciousness flickered back, a painful return to a reality shrouded in darkness. He lay in a chamber draped in tattered black curtains, the air thick with the scent of stale incense and something else... something acrid and unsettling. Flickering crimson candles, strategically placed on rough-hewn tables, cast dancing shadows, painting the room in a grotesque, infernal glow. He attempted to rise, his limbs heavy, his mind clouded. He scanned the chamber, desperately seeking an escape, a glimmer of hope in the suffocating gloom.

Before he could formulate a plan, a figure emerged from the shadows – a woman clad in a long, flowing robe of deepest black. "My name is Raven Locke," she announced, her voice a silken whisper that somehow cut through the oppressive silence. "And I am here to... engage in a dialogue. Be seated, Caleb." The command was not harsh, but it carried an undercurrent of absolute authority.

"How... how do you know my name?" Caleb stammered, his voice raspy and uncertain.

"You will find, Caleb," Raven purred, circling him like a predator assessing its prey, "that I possess a certain... *insight*... into your affairs, and those of your... associates."

He sank, defeated, into a rickety wooden chair beside a small, scarred table. Raven remained standing, a looming presence behind him, a position of subtle dominance.

"Let us discuss the crystal," she began, her voice smooth and insinuating, "the one your team so recently... *discovered*. Its location. Its properties. Its *purpose*."

"I... I don't know," Caleb stammered, the lie a fragile shield. "I was taken before we could properly analyze the data. It was... a source of energy, perhaps. Beyond that... I am ignorant. You have the wrong individual for such questions."

"Come now, Caleb," Raven chided, her voice a silken caress laced with menace. "You were present. You *witnessed* its power. The readings... they are etched in your mind, however faintly. I can *sense* them. You must possess *some* understanding, some inkling of its true nature."

"I truly don't," Caleb insisted, but a tremor of doubt betrayed him. "It was unlike anything I've ever encountered. The light... it was blinding, yet... cold. And the feeling... as if it were *aware*, watching us. It was... profoundly disturbing."

Raven probed, her subtle magic seeking entry into his mind, a violation he could feel but not fully comprehend. She sifted through his surface thoughts, his fears, his fleeting impressions, finding little of concrete value.

"We shall revisit this conversation, Caleb," she said, her voice a chilling promise. "And for your sake, you will cultivate a more... *forthcoming* disposition. Your continued existence depends upon your cooperation."

With a swirl of her black robes, Raven swept from the chamber, the heavy wooden door echoing shut behind her, a resounding punctuation mark to her threat. She proceeded down a long, dimly lit corridor, the air growing heavier, more oppressive with each step. She reached a larger chamber, the private domain of the Grand Imperator, Lord Valerius. She bowed low, a gesture of absolute subservience.

"My Lord," she reported, her voice carefully neutral, "the prisoner possesses limited knowledge. We acted prematurely. He knows only that the artifact is a crystal of considerable power, possibly a relic of divine origin. He suspects its potential, but lacks specifics. Securing it, however, would undoubtedly earn us the profound gratitude of the Shivara."

"Indeed," Valerius rumbled, his voice a deep, resonant growl. "We must acquire this crystal. And quickly. We shall exploit this captive. Use him as a conduit, a living instrument to extract the information we require from his leader. Command Nightshade. Have her devise a spell, a ritual, to unlock his mind and make him our unwitting spy."

"It shall be done, My Lord."

Raven departed, her footsteps echoing in the oppressive silence, and made her way towards the Ritualist's sanctum. Deep within the bowels of the Order's hidden fortress, a place where darkness reigned supreme and the air crackled with forbidden energies, she found Nightshade.

"Lord Valerius demands your expertise," Raven announced, her voice crisp and devoid of emotion. "We require a bewitchment. A mortal mind must be subtly... *reconfigured*... to serve as our informant, unknowingly betraying the secrets of his comrades. Speed is of the essence."

"Bring the mortal to me," Nightshade replied, her voice a rasping whisper, "and I shall weave a potion, a draught of subtle dominion, that will bend his will to our purpose."

Raven issued the order, and guards, their faces impassive and devoid of empathy, delivered Caleb into the Ritualist's hands. Within moments, the dark work was complete. Caleb, his mind subtly altered, his memories fragmented, was released back into the city, an unwitting puppet of the Order of the Veil, a ticking clock counting down to the moment of betrayal. The game had entered a new, more dangerous phase.

Thorne, driven by a steely resolve, initiated the search for Eira. A location, however vague, was a foothold in the vastness of the unknown. He offered a silent prayer for guidance, for the strength to overcome whatever obstacles the enigmatic Aurora Initiative presented. There *had* to be a way. The fleet, a symphony of controlled power, sliced through the tapestry of the multiverse, then, with a practiced maneuver, folded space itself, emerging into the orbit around Solara. Thorne immediately shrouded the vessels in a cloaking field, a veil of invisibility against both the primitive sensors of this world and the ever-watchful gaze of the Shivara. He hand-picked a squad of his most elite warriors, each a veteran of countless battles, their loyalty and skill unquestioned. Their destination: Acarcis.

The city was a sprawling behemoth, a concrete jungle of towering skyscrapers and cramped dwellings, a testament to a civilization both advanced and deeply stratified. Across the vast urban expanse, one structure dominated the skyline – a monolith of steel and glass, crowned with a landing platform. The Aurora Initiative. Thorne, his senses heightened, directed the pilot towards the target, a silent command ensuring the cloaking field remained flawlessly intact. They were ghosts, phantoms, slipping unseen into the heart of the enemy's territory.

Activating their personal cloaking devices, Thorne and his team transitioned from the vessel to the building's interior, moving with the practiced grace of seasoned infiltrators. They were shadows, whispers in the corridors, their presence undetectable. Level by level, they navigated the structure, a silent, methodical sweep, observing, assessing, searching for their quarry. Finally, their patience was rewarded. In a secure laboratory, Dr. Thompson and Dr. Singh, the architects of this perplexing mystery, were identified, their heads bent in intense concentration over a cascade of data streams – the secrets of the Keystone, and perhaps, the key to Eira's fate. The tension was a taut wire, stretched to the breaking point. The moment of confrontation was at hand. Every second counted.

As Elijah entered his private office, a sanctuary of supposed security, Thorne materialized behind him, a silent emergence from the veiled realm of invisibility. Elijah, startled by the impossible intrusion, spun around, a gasp of shock escaping his lips.

"Who are you?" he demanded, his voice a mixture of alarm and disbelief. "How did you penetrate our defenses?"

"I am Thorne," the intruder stated, his voice calm yet resonant with authority, "an emissary of the Bramah, serving the Elder Gods. Guardians of the Sacred Keystones."

"Gods?" Elijah scoffed, a flicker of skepticism crossing his face. "Keystones? These are meaningless terms. What is your purpose here?"

"You possess a mortal," Thorne continued, his gaze unwavering, "a young woman named Eira. She resonates with the frequencies of the Keystones – a phenomenon of profound significance. You also, recently, acquired a... sample... of a Keystone itself."

"Is that the designation for the crystalline structure we discovered?" Elijah inquired, his scientific curiosity piqued, despite the unsettling circumstances. "Its function? Is it merely a source of energy?"

"It is far more than that," Thorne corrected, his voice taking on a tone of grave importance. "Keystones are the foundation of existence, the anchors of balance across the vast multiverse. Countless worlds depend upon their integrity."

"And your intentions?" Elijah pressed, his suspicion growing.

"We must secure the girl," Thorne declared, his voice leaving no room for negotiation. "Transport her to the Bramah stronghold. To study her unique connection to the Keystones. To fulfill the mandate of the Elder Gods, and, crucially, to protect her from the Shivara and the machinations of the Dark Gods. We must depart *immediately*."

Elijah hesitated, weighing his options. Then, a calculated decision. "I have a condition. Myself and my associate, Dr. Maya Singh, must accompany you. The girl has formed an attachment. She trusts us. Our presence will facilitate a smoother... transition."

Thorne considered the request for a fleeting moment, then nodded curtly. "Agreed. Lead the way. *Now.*" The reluctance was palpable, but the urgency of the situation superseded all other considerations.

Elijah led Thorne to his laboratory, signaling to Dr. Singh to join them. The three then proceeded to Eira's quarters. A brief knock, and the door opened, revealing Eira, her expression a mixture of apprehension and fragile hope.

Elijah met her gaze, his voice carefully modulated. "Eira, this individual is... of considerable importance. We must accompany him on a journey to a different location. Your safety will be assured there."

"Where?" Eira asked, her voice barely a whisper.

"A place of sanctuary," Elijah replied, his tone reassuring, yet evasive. "A stronghold, protected from all threats. We can continue our research there, uninterrupted. But we must act with haste."

"Alright, Dr. Thompson," Eira agreed, her trust in the scientist, however misplaced, overriding her lingering unease.

Together, the group – a fragile alliance forged in the crucible of necessity – hurried towards Thorne's concealed vessel. Once aboard, the ship ascended with breathtaking speed, leaving the familiar world behind, embarking on a perilous journey towards an uncertain future, the fate of the multiverse hanging precariously in the balance.

Within the radiant heart of Elysium, the celestial domain of the Elder Gods, a realm beyond mortal comprehension, Elyon, God of Creation, Harmony, and Balance – the radiant shepherd of the cosmic flock – convened with Kronos, God of Time and Order, his essence a tapestry woven with the threads of eternity.

They stood upon a precipice of shimmering light, overlooking the boundless panorama of existence, a tapestry of swirling galaxies and nascent worlds. Elyon's voice, a symphony of creation itself, broke the sacred silence. *"Do you perceive, within the delicate threads of fate, the triumph of balance? Or will the shadow of chaos ultimately consume all that we have wrought?"*

Kronos, his gaze fixed upon the intricate dance of time, his voice a resonant echo of ages past and yet to come, responded, *"Ah, if only we could pierce the veil of the Void, that impenetrable shroud woven by the Dark Gods. To glimpse their machinations, to anticipate their strikes... surely, there must exist a means."*

"They crafted their obfuscation with cruel cunning, brother," Elyon acknowledged, a trace of sorrow in his divine voice.

A question, hanging heavy with the weight of cosmic responsibility, drifted between them. *"Shall we extend our hand to the Bramah, offer direct aid in their perilous endeavors?"*

Kronos, his gaze still lost in the labyrinth of time, answered with measured deliberation. *"The hour of intervention may yet arrive. But for now, we must remain vigilant, observers of the unfolding drama. Our presence, a beacon in the encroaching darkness, must suffice."*

And so, the two divine beings, architects of reality, guardians of existence, maintained their celestial vigil, their gaze fixed upon the fragile tapestry of creation, patiently awaiting the inevitable moment when the Dark Gods would unleash their fury, the moment when the delicate balance would teeter on the precipice of oblivion. The silence of Elysium was not the silence of inaction, but the profound, expectant stillness before a cosmic storm, a testament to the unwavering faith, the quiet hope, and the awesome, unfathomable mystery that lay at the heart of divine power.

Deep within the festering heart of the Void, a realm of absolute nothingness and primordial chaos, the domain of the Dark Gods, Zarathos,

God of Destruction, Chaos, and Darkness – the malevolent tyrant of this blighted realm – paced before his throne of obsidian and bone. A furious tempest raged within him, a reflection of the chaotic energies he commanded. With a roar that ripped through the very fabric of the Void, a sound of pure, unadulterated rage, he summoned Lyraea, Goddess of Madness and Discord, to his presence.

She materialized before him, a whirlwind of fractured sanity and malicious intent, and prostrated herself, a groveling display of forced subservience. ***"Speak, my Lord. How may I serve your glorious wrath?"***

"The Elder Gods!" Zarathos spat the name like a curse, his voice a venomous growl. ***"What whispers of their pathetic schemes have reached your twisted ears?"***

"Mortals, on the insignificant dust mote called Solara," Lyraea reported, her voice a sibilant hiss, ***"have stumbled upon a Keystone of considerable power. It may be the source of the recent disruption. The Bramah, those self-righteous lapdogs of the Ancients, are undoubtedly aware. Their next move will be to secure it. We should strike first, seize the Keystone, and twist its power to our own ends."***

"Do not presume to instruct me, Lyraea!" Zarathos roared, his eyes blazing with infernal fire. ***"The strategy of the Dark Gods is mine to dictate! Your place is to obey, not to offer unsolicited counsel."***

"My apologies, Great Lord," Lyraea groveled, her voice laced with feigned contrition. ***"My zeal to serve overstepped its bounds."***

Zarathos, his fury momentarily appeased, dismissed her with a contemptuous wave of his hand. Lyraea vanished, leaving the God of Destruction alone with his seething thoughts. The Keystone. The Bramah. The meddling Elder Gods. A plan began to form, a tapestry of destruction and conquest, woven with threads of malice and fueled by an insatiable hunger for power. The time for subtle machinations was over. The time for open war, for the ultimate annihilation of all that opposed the Dark Gods, was at hand. The universe would tremble, and all creation would drown in a tide of glorious chaos.

As Thorne's fleet approached the Bramah stronghold, Elijah's jaw practically dropped. He'd never seen anything *remotely* like it. This wasn't just some building; it was a colossal structure, defying gravity, hovering effortlessly above the planet's surface like something out of a dream. They docked alongside what looked like *hundreds* of other ships, a mind-boggling display of power. Elijah couldn't even begin to guess how many soldiers were stationed here. It was completely beyond anything he could have imagined.

Thorne guided them through the stronghold, leading them towards Lila's laboratory, where Aethon was waiting. After a quick greeting, Thorne turned to introduce the newcomers.

"Sir, these are the individuals we discussed. Dr. Elijah Thompson and Dr. Maya Singh, from the Aurora Initiative. And this," he gestured towards Eira, "is Eira, the young woman we've been seeking."

"Welcome, all of you," Aethon said, a warm, genuine smile on his face.

Elijah and Maya were utterly speechless, staring around at the lab. The equipment here... it wasn't just advanced; it was almost *magical*, defying their understanding of science. Lila, meanwhile, ushered Eira towards an examination table.

It was then that Eira saw him – Erebus. A knowing smile spread across her face, a silent acknowledgment of the strange, inexplicable bond they shared. This was the voice in her head, the one who had warned her.

Erebus returned her smile, and, impossibly, his voice echoed in her mind. *"Welcome to... wherever this is. I'm still trying to figure out what's going on. They haven't exactly been forthcoming with information. But... I don't think they're bad guys."*

"I got the same feeling about the people from the Aurora Initiative," Eira responded mentally, *"though I'm not entirely sure what their ultimate goals are."*

"Do they know about your crystal?"

"No," Eira thought back. *"I've managed to keep it hidden."*

"Be careful," Erebus warned. *"The equipment here... it's sensitive. They'll detect it, even if you try to... well, you'll see."*

"How can you... do that?" Eira asked, bewildered.

"You mean make it disappear? Haven't you experimented with its capabilities?"

"The only thing I've discovered is that it can render me invisible," Eira admitted.

"There's so much more," Erebus replied, a hint of excitement in his mental voice. *"Maybe, if we get the chance, we can explore its full potential. If they give us the opportunity."*

Lila, ever the observant scientist, motioned for Eira to lie back on the examination table. The scans began, and it wasn't long before the instruments registered the familiar signature of the crystal, hidden within Eira's pocket. Lila requested to see it, and Eira, with a mixture of trust and apprehension, complied, handing over her precious secret. The mystery, it seemed, was only just beginning to unravel.

Dr. Singh watched with a mixture of intense scientific curiosity and growing apprehension as Lila, following her instructions, slowly brought the two Keystone shards closer. The air in the chamber, deep within the Bramah stronghold, thickened with a subtle, almost imperceptible energy. Eira and Erebus, seated across from each other on raised platforms of polished obsidian, began to react. A low hum, *too deep to be audible, yet undeniably present*, resonated within their minds, growing in intensity with each passing moment.

It was a sound Eira vaguely, terrifyingly, remembered from *the shrine on Elyria, deep beneath the great city, where she had stood with Dr. Thompson and Dr. Singh before the Prime Keystone itself*. A tremor ran through both young people, a visible manifestation of the unseen forces at play. Dr. Singh, standing at a console displaying intricate runic patterns that pulsed with faint light, her initial excitement tempered by a prickle of unease, gestured sharply to the other Bramah attendants, her eyes fixed on the shifting patterns displaying Eira and Erebus's rapidly escalating vital signs.

Deep within their shared consciousness, a presence stirred. It felt ancient, immense, and utterly alien.

"I live!"

The two words, raw and resonant with impossible power, echoed not in their ears, but in the very core of their beings, sparking a primal fear intertwined with an almost unbearable wonder. What was this entity? What did its awakening portend? Eira, her eyes wide with terror and confusion, looked desperately towards Aethon, a silent plea for help etched on her face. The Bramah leader, his own face a mask of controlled concern, responded instantly. He moved to the two mortals, gently but firmly embracing them, a gesture of protection and reassurance.

He gave Lila a curt nod, a silent command. Lila, her hands trembling slightly, quickly separated the shards. The instant they broke contact, a shockwave of unseen energy erupted, a silent explosion that ripped through the chamber. This was no mere ritual. The pulse, invisible to the naked eye, blasted outwards, extending far beyond the confines of the stronghold. Across the vast expanse of the multiverse, worlds shuddered, timelines fractured and reformed, and the delicate balance that had held for eons was irrevocably disrupted.

The Keystone, in some terrifying, incomprehensible way, had activated again. A wave of cold dread washed over Aethon. They had witnessed something profound, something potentially catastrophic.

Guardians of the Keystones: Echoes

Chapter Six

The hum of machinery was a constant, almost unnoticed backdrop to the work at the Aurora Initiative. Data streams, complex and indecipherable to the untrained eye, flowed across the monitors, meticulously analyzed and categorized. Caleb Reyes *staggered* into the lab, his eyes wide and unfocused, a look of profound bewilderment etched on his face. He seemed to be adrift, lost in a familiar place that had suddenly become alien. At the central console, Dr. Adrian Volkov, *a figure Caleb didn't recognize,* was immersed in the data flowing from the Keystone, his brow furrowed in concentration. The sight of *strangers – unfamiliar faces, unknown names* – working on *his* project sent a jolt of disorientation through Caleb. This wasn't right. This wasn't *his* team.

"Where... where is Dr. Thompson? And Dr. Singh?" His voice was hesitant, a tremor of uncertainty underlining each word.

Volkov glanced up, his expression unreadable. "Dr. Thompson retired over five years ago. Dr. Singh is engaged in a... *separate* initiative." The way he said "separate" suggested layers of meaning, implications Caleb couldn't grasp.

"No," Caleb insisted, his voice gaining a desperate edge. "No, Dr. Thompson *leads* this project. He *always* has."

Volkov's gaze sharpened, a flicker of something – annoyance? suspicion? – crossing his face. "Caleb, are you feeling alright? Dr. Singh has overseen this project since Dr. Thompson's departure. *Five years*, Caleb."

The words struck Caleb like a physical blow. Five years? How could that be? It felt like *yesterday* he was working alongside Thompson, discussing the preliminary findings, the *potential* of the Keystone. A wave of nausea washed over him. Had he hit his head? Was this some elaborate, cruel delusion? The lab, the equipment, the faces... they swam before his eyes, familiar yet distorted, like a reflection in rippling water. He pressed his hands to his temples, trying to force his mind to make sense, to grasp some solid truth in this shifting reality. *The crystal*. Somehow, the thought of the Keystone, its enigmatic energy, its *promise*, cut through the fog of confusion. It was the only thing that felt real, the only thing that mattered. He *had* to understand it.

Dr. Volkov's gaze lingered on Caleb, a flicker of something *unreadable* in his eyes – concern, perhaps, but tinged with something colder, more calculating. "You should go to the infirmary, Reyes. Get yourself checked. We need everyone operating at peak efficiency. If you're unwell, *rest*. We can't afford any... *distractions*." The emphasis on "rest" and "distractions" felt less like a suggestion and more like a veiled threat.

"Yes, sir." The words were automatic, a reflex.

Caleb stumbled back towards the lift, the metal doors closing with a *hiss* that echoed the growing unease in his gut. The infirmary. The *last* place he needed to be. The crystal... he *had* to understand it. The compulsion was a physical ache, a driving force that drowned out everything else. He didn't understand *why* he needed to know, only that it was the most important thing in the world, a matter of *life and death*, though he couldn't have said whose.

The visit to the infirmary was a charade, a hurried performance of normalcy. He feigned cooperation, answered questions with rote responses, and within minutes, he was walking back to the lab, a fabricated clean bill of health clutched in his hand. Back in the lab, he forced a mask of casual interest, burying his disorientation and the terrifying gaps in his memory beneath a layer of feigned normalcy. He *had* to blend in. He *had* to learn. The fact that he didn't recognize a single face, that this team was a complete mystery, was a secret he guarded with desperate care.

The data scrolling across the screens was breathtaking, almost terrifying in its implications. The Keystone's power readings were astronomical, defying all known physics, emanating from a source that remained stubbornly, impossibly, *undefined*. He approached Dr. Volkov, trying to sound casual, as if his very existence wasn't a fragile lie.

"Sir, do we have any idea... what it *is*?"

Volkov barely glanced up, his eyes fixed on the swirling patterns of data. "There's some form of inscription on the far wall. A language, apparently, but unlike anything in our databases. Utterly unknown. *Fascinating*." The word was spoken with a chilling detachment, as if he were discussing an interesting specimen rather than an object of potentially universe-altering power.

"And...what's holding it? Why can't it be moved?"

"Unknown. It appears to be... anchored. To spacetime itself. The planet *orbits* the crystal, Reyes. Think about the implications of *that*."

Caleb backed away, feigning a need to examine other data displays. A cold, almost primal urge was pulling at him, a desperate need to *escape*, to get *out* of the building. He fought it, reason telling him it was madness, but the feeling intensified, a silent scream in the back of his mind. He glanced around, ensuring no one was paying him particular attention. Then, with a sudden, almost involuntary movement, he slipped out onto the docking platform.

The air outside was thick with a strange stillness. Then, the darkness *shifted*. A black mist, impossibly dense, coalesced before him, swirling and thickening until it formed a ragged, *light-devouring* portal. Caleb stood frozen, his mind emptied of thought, a puppet waiting for its strings to be pulled. From the depths of the portal, Raven Locke and Nightshade emerged, their presence radiating a palpable menace.

"Report." The command was a rasp, devoid of warmth or humanity.

Caleb, his will completely subsumed, recounted everything he had learned about the crystal, his voice a monotone drone. Raven and Nightshade exchanged a look, a silent communication that spoke of ambition and the cruel satisfaction of a plan unfolding.

"The Dark Gods will be *pleased*. Forget, *worm*." The word "worm" was spat with utter contempt.

Nightshade began to chant, a guttural incantation that seemed to claw at the edges of reality. Caleb stood motionless, his eyes glazed over, his mind a blank slate. Raven and Nightshade retreated into the swirling blackness, the portal snapping shut behind them, leaving no trace of their presence. Caleb, his purpose fulfilled, his memory wiped, turned and walked back inside, *a hollow shell*, and took the lift down to his quarters. He moved without thought, without will, a mere automaton. He collapsed onto his bed and fell into a sleep so deep it was almost a coma. His usefulness to the Order of the Veil was, for the moment, at an end.

The echo of that impossible voice – *"I live!"* – vanished, leaving a ringing silence in the chamber that was somehow heavier, more profound, than before. Dust motes danced in the strange, still air. Eira gasped, pressing trembling hands to her temples, the phantom vibration of the mental shout still resonating deep within her skull. Across from her, Erebus swayed, his eyes wide with a terror that mirrored her own. Had anyone else heard it?

Around them, the controlled environment of the Bramah laboratory had dissolved into stunned immobility. Dr. Singh staggered back a step, her hand flying to her mouth. Bramah attendants, usually paragons of stoic efficiency, gripped consoles, their knuckles white, faces frozen in disbelief. The intricate runic patterns on the displays flickered erratically, pulsing with discordant light.

Then, Lila broke the spell. With a choked cry, she lunged towards her primary console, fingers flying across the interface with desperate speed. Symbols flashed across the screen – star charts warping, energy signatures spiking into impossible reds, complex waveforms dissolving into static. Alerts began to chime, low at first, then rising in a cacophony of synthesized panic.

"Aethon..." Lila whispered, her voice tight, unrecognizable. She didn't look away from the cascade of catastrophic data. "The... the readings... multiple sectors... timelines are..." She trailed off, shaking her head, unable to articulate the scale of it.

Aethon was already moving towards her, his gaze sweeping from the chaotic displays to the two mortals, still trembling, then to the now-separated Keystone shards resting innocuously on their stands. The connection, the horrifying implication of cause and effect, hit him with the force of a physical blow. That pulse... hadn't been contained.

"Impossible," he breathed, the word barely audible. He saw it on the screens now – representations of reality fraying at the edges, dimensions bleeding into one another like watercolors left in the rain. What had they done? What had they unleashed?

His voice, when it came, cut through the rising panic like sharpened steel. "Guards!" Heads snapped towards him. "Take them. Separate rooms – different *wings* of the stronghold. Keep those shards *apart*! Now!"

He gripped the edge of Lila's console, the cool metal grounding him against the wave of cold dread washing through him. The guards moved instantly, flanking Eira and Erebus, who offered no resistance, still reeling from the psychic backlash and the sudden, terrifying shift in atmosphere. As they were led away in opposite directions, the only sounds in the chamber were the insistent, blaring alarms from Lila's console and the heavy, unsteady rhythm of Aethon's own breathing. The stronghold, moments before a place of controlled scientific inquiry, now felt like the epicenter of a potentially universe-shattering catastrophe. The consequences were unknown, unpredictable, and utterly terrifying.

The blaring alarms gradually subsided under Lila's frantic manipulations, replaced by an oppressive silence broken only by the frantic clicking of her console and the low, ominous hum of stressed machinery. Order felt a universe away; the data streams flooding her screens were pure chaos – timelines flickering like dying stars, dimensional boundaries fraying into static, causality indexes plummeting into red zones across countless sectors.

Elijah stood near a secondary display showing raw energy metrics that defied physics, his face pale, muttering under his breath, "...impossible energy cascade... breaching known constants..." He finally turned towards Lila, his voice strained, barely audible above the lab's low thrum. "Lila... the pulse... *what* just happened?"

Lila didn't look away from the swirling vortex of multiversal damage reports on her main screen. Her voice was tight, brittle. "Activation. The shard proximity triggered a resonance cascade... directly impacting the Prime Keystone." She gestured vaguely, helplessly, at the horrifying mosaic of data. "The effects... they're not local. They're... everywhere."

"Everywhere?" Elijah moved closer, peering over her shoulder at the incomprehensible disaster unfolding visually. "But... Keystones stabilize... they don't..."

"They *are* the structure, Elijah!" Lila snapped, finally tearing her gaze away to meet his, her eyes wide with a terror that mirrored his own nascent dread. "They *are* reality. We just slammed the foundations with... *that*." She jabbed a finger towards the now empty examination area where Eira and Erebus had been. "This stronghold's shielding absorbed the immediate wave, but *out there*..." Her voice trailed off, the implication hanging heavy in the charged air.

A cold fist clenched around Elijah's heart. "Out there?" he echoed, his throat suddenly dry. "Our home? Acarcis? Solara?"

Lila's hands flew across the console again, initiating targeted diagnostic sweeps, overlaying their origin coordinates onto the fluctuating instability maps. The seconds stretched, each click of the console a hammer blow against the silence. Then, an image resolved – Solara's systemic coordinates, overlaid with pulsing, angry red warnings indicating severe temporal and dimensional instability. Lila let out a sharp, broken gasp.

"It was hit, Elijah," she confirmed, her voice dropping to a horrified whisper. "Solara's timeline... it's tagged. Unstable."

Elijah gripped the console edge, his knuckles white. "Unstable how? Define the parameters! Is it... erased?"

Lila shook her head, eyes glued to the fluctuating readings that refused to resolve into coherent data. "The interference patterns...the temporal echoes are too chaotic. It's impossible to determine the *extent* of the alterations from here." She finally looked up at him, her expression bleak. "It's changed, Elijah. Your universe... your world... it's been altered. How much... we simply don't know."

Elijah turned slowly, his gaze searching for Maya across the now-silent lab. Their eyes met, and the unspoken fear passed between them – a shared, sickening dread. The world they had left behind, the colleagues, the city...what did their pursuit of knowledge just cost? Was there anything left to return to?

The air in the deepest sanctum of the Order of the Veil was cold, thick with the metallic tang of old blood and the cloying sweetness of corrupted incense. Shadows clung to the roughly carved stone walls like living things, seeming to writhe in sympathy with the guttural chanting emanating from the chamber's center. There, before a grotesque obsidian altar dedicated to Zarathos, Lord Valerius knelt, his form barely discernible amidst the oppressive darkness, lost in communion with his dark patrons.

Raven Locke moved like a phantom, her black robes blending seamlessly with the gloom, Nightshade a deeper, unsettling silhouette trailing silently in her wake. They stopped at the edge of the ritual space, hesitant to break the fragile connection Valerius maintained. But the news couldn't wait.

Raven took a shallow breath, the air feeling unnaturally heavy in her lungs. "My Lord Valerius," her voice was a carefully pitched whisper, designed not to startle but firm enough to penetrate his concentration. "Forgive this intrusion. Urgent intelligence requires your attention... intelligence for the Shivara."

The chanting stopped abruptly. The temperature in the chamber plummeted. Valerius didn't turn immediately; instead, the shadows around him seemed to deepen, coalesce. When his head finally twisted towards them, his eyes glowed with a faint, malevolent crimson, pinning them in place.

"You interrupt my supplications... *why*?" The voice wasn't just angry; it grated like tombstones scraping together, heavy with displeasure and restrained power.

"The opportunity, My Lord," Raven kept her gaze respectfully lowered but her voice steady, "is too significant to delay." Nightshade remained utterly still, radiating a cold, watchful presence.

A low growl rumbled in Valerius's chest. "Report."

"Our asset within the Aurora Initiative confirms their findings," Raven stated concisely. "A crystal artifact, immense power readings... consistent with a Keystone. Located in a shrine beneath an ancient city, far from their territory. More importantly... they have secured a young female. She resonates with the artifact. They believe she can wield it."

The crimson glow in Valerius's eyes intensified, the anger shifting, sharpening into avaricious interest. The air crackled faintly. "A mortal... capable of wielding a Keystone?" He rose slowly, the shadows peeling away from him like shed skin. "The Shivara will desire this... *instrument*. Does Aurora hold the girl now?"

"Yes, My Lord. Within their primary facility."

A predatory smile stretched Valerius's lips, making his face seem even more skull-like in the flickering candlelight. "Excellent. Prepare the Faceless." The name alone evoked whispers of silent death and impossible infiltration. "They will penetrate the Aurora facility. Retrieve the girl. Bring her to us. Unseen. Unheard."

"It shall be done, My Lord," Raven affirmed.

Valerius turned back towards the altar, his attention already returning to his dark communion, the mortal agents dismissed from his thoughts. Raven and Nightshade exchanged a brief, almost imperceptible glance – an understanding passing between them – before melting back into the oppressive darkness of the corridor. Their steps were silent, purposeful, heading towards the shadowed cloister where the Order's most terrifying assassins awaited their command. A new, dark strand was being woven into the already tangled web of the cosmic conflict.

Guardians of the Keystones: Echoes

Chapter Seven

Aethon knelt before the Cosmic Tree, the ethereal light from its shimmering leaves doing little to pierce the gloom that had settled over his spirit. He rested his forehead against the ancient, living bark, the smooth surface cool beneath his skin, but offered no comfort. The low, chaotic thrum of unstable energies echoing from Lila's distant lab felt like a physical manifestation of his failure. *Chaos unleashed.* Under his command. Under his watch.

Had he been wrong? Had they moved too quickly, blinded by the need to understand the shards, the mortals, the connection? He traced a spiraling pattern on the Tree's trunk, a gesture learned millennia ago when seeking simple clarity. Now, clarity felt impossibly far away. The balance...the delicate, intricate balance the Elder Gods entrusted him to maintain...felt shattered, the pieces scattered across realities by the very experiment he had sanctioned.

A wave of profound weariness washed over him, the weight of ages pressing down. He remembered accepting the mantle of leadership – a burden he never truly desired, thrust upon him after the First Shadow War. The previous leader, valiant but too rigid, had faltered. Aethon's own strategy then, sacrificing worlds on the periphery to save the core, had been agonizing, controversial...but *necessary*. He had felt the grim certainty of the calculations then, the cold logic of balance demanding a terrible price.

But was this the same? Was this catastrophe born of necessity, or merely...error? Hubris? The whispers from the Tree had been fragmented then, desperate, yet guiding. Now, before the activation, there had been Nyx's cryptic warning, yes, but no clear directive *against* the experiment, only caution. Had he misinterpreted? Or simply failed to heed the underlying warning?

He was Aethon, the eldest, born from the first echoes of creation alongside Lirien, attuned since inception to the delicate equilibrium of existence. He had spent eons meditating here, at these very roots, feeling the pulse of countless realities, striving to understand the harmony the Elder Gods embodied. The irony wasn't lost on him – the scholar of balance presiding over an act that had potentially sown unparalleled discord. Lirien, ever the diplomat, might have urged more patience, more negotiation...perhaps Lirien would have been right this time.

He closed his eyes, the shimmering light of the Tree filtering through his eyelids like tears of starlight. The weight felt unbearable. He needed...not just answers, but solace. Understanding. He focused his will, his weary spirit reaching out, forming a silent prayer not just to the Tree, but through it, towards the source of all harmony itself.

"Elyon," his thought was a ragged whisper into the heartwood of reality, "Father of Creation, Shepherd of Balance...grant me wisdom. Grant me strength. Have I...have *we*...irrevocably broken what You charged us to protect?"

He remained kneeling, head bowed, awaiting a response that might never come, the silence profound, the weight of a fractured multiverse resting heavily upon his ancient shoulders.

The confirmation that Solara's timeline was "unstable" hung in the charged air of the Bramah lab like a death sentence. Elijah met Maya's horrified gaze across the chaotic displays. The unspoken question resonated between them: *What did unstable mean? What was left?*

"Thorne," Elijah's voice was low, tight with urgency, barely masking the tremor beneath. "We need transport. Back to the Initiative. Immediately."

Maya nodded, her expression grim. "We have to see." *If there's anything left to see,* the unspoken words echoed.

Thorne regarded them for a moment, his ancient eyes seeming to weigh their desperation against cosmic necessity. He gave a curt nod. "This way." He led them from the chaotic lab to a large, circular chamber dominated by a raised, glowing pad. The sheer scale and alien nature of the Bramah technology, which had seemed wondrous before, now felt oppressive, emphasizing their own sudden smallness. Thorne handed Elijah a small, metallic object. "Communicator. Standard frequency. For Bramah contact only." He gestured towards the pad. "Step into the center. Prepare yourselves."

They hesitated for only a fraction of a second, clutching equipment cases like shields, before stepping onto the glowing surface with their anxious team members. Light flared, swirling around them with dizzying speed, accompanied by a disorienting pressure. Then, abruptly, they were standing on the familiar landing port high atop the Aurora Initiative headquarters.

The air tasted the same. The city sprawl below looked, at first glance, unchanged. But something felt...*off*. A subtle dissonance in the ambient hum of the building? A different security drone sweeping past than the model they'd used? Elijah exchanged a cautious glance with Maya. They proceeded carefully, moving through the corridors towards their lab sector, every familiar corner now viewed with suspicion, searching for overt signs of alteration.

They didn't have to search long. As they rounded the final corridor, a man Elijah had never seen before stepped out from the lab entrance, smiling warmly, primarily at Maya. He had an air of confident authority.

"Dr. Singh! Welcome back!" the man greeted, his tone familiar and collegial. "Excellent timing, we're about to analyze the probe data. Trip go smoothly?" He then seemed to notice Elijah, his smile faltering slightly into polite surprise. "Dr. Thompson? Are you visiting today, sir? Always good to see you. How's retirement treating you?"

Retirement? The word slammed into Elijah with physical force. He felt Maya tense beside him, and saw her force a neutral, slightly strained smile.

"Dr...Volkov," Maya replied, her voice remarkably steady, though Elijah caught the slight hesitation before the name. "Yes, the trip was...informative. Dr. Thompson was providing some historical consultation." She quickly turned to their team, her voice regaining its professional crispness. "Secure the equipment in staging bay three, begin diagnostic checks on the sensor arrays."

As the team hurried off, relieved to escape the sudden tension, Maya turned back to Volkov. "Historical context is always valuable, Adrian." *Adrian?* "Perhaps Dr. Thompson would appreciate seeing the progress you've made on the crystal analysis since...well, since he left?"

"Of course," Volkov beamed, seemingly oblivious to the undercurrents, gesturing them towards the lab. "We've had some fascinating breakthroughs since Dr. Singh took over the project five years ago..."

Five years. Elijah felt a cold dread wash over him as he walked beside Maya, listening to Volkov describe advancements and personnel changes that were utterly alien. He forced himself to nod, to appear engaged, while his mind reeled. This wasn't just unstable. This was wrong. Terribly, fundamentally wrong. He caught Maya's eye again – the same panicked confusion mirrored there. They were back, but they weren't home. Not anymore.

The lab buzzed with an unfamiliar rhythm, filled with faces Elijah didn't recognize alongside equipment that seemed subtly, jarringly different. He pulled Maya into a small, empty observation alcove overlooking the main floor, the glass hopefully muffling their words.

"Five years, Maya?" His voice was a harsh whisper, disbelief warring with dawning fear. "Retirement? Volkov in charge? What *happened* here?"

Maya pressed her fingers to her temples, shaking her head slightly. "I don't know, Elijah. Adrian Volkov... I remember him, peripherally, from Xenobotanical years ago. Competent, ambitious... but running *this* project? And reporting to *me*?" She met his gaze, her own confusion mirroring his. "That pulse... Lila said it altered timelines. This... this must be the result."

"Altered is an understatement," Elijah muttered, glancing back towards the lab floor where Volkov was overseeing the analysis. "He accepted my presence far too easily. We're exposed here, Maya. Compromised."

"We need access," Maya said, her voice low and determined. "To the systems, the logs... we have to understand the divergence point. And we need to analyze the data we brought back from... from the Bramah." She hesitated. "Volkov seems to accept my authority, for now. Maybe... maybe we use that? Frame you as a specialist, brought back to consult on this specific energy signature due to its unique nature?"

Elijah considered it, grimacing. It felt thin, dangerous. "It's a risk. He seems... observant. But we don't have many options." He took a deep breath. "Alright. Let's try. But stay alert. Watch him."

They stepped back into the main lab, projecting an air of professional calm they didn't feel. Maya approached Volkov, who was intently studying a complex energy waveform on a large display.

"Adrian," Maya began, her tone measured, "the preliminary sensor data from our expedition confirms the energy signature is... unprecedented. Its complexity requires analysis beyond our standard protocols."

Volkov turned, a flicker of intense curiosity in his eyes. "Indeed? More potent than anticipated?"

"Significantly," Maya confirmed. "Given the potential implications, I've asked Dr. Thompson to come out of retirement temporarily to consult directly on this project. His foundational work in high-energy resonance is unparalleled." She deliberately framed it as her decision, leveraging the authority Volkov seemed to grant her.

Volkov's gaze shifted to Elijah, a slow, assessing look that lingered a moment too long. Then, a smooth smile spread across his face. "Dr. Thompson? A surprise, certainly, but a welcome one. Your expertise would be invaluable, Doctor. Of course, Maya, any resources you require. Consider him fully reinstated for the duration." The acceptance felt too easy, the smile not quite reaching his eyes.

Elijah forced a nod, resisting the urge to demand answers. "Thank you, Dr. Volkov. The data requires immediate attention." He turned to his original team members, who looked bewildered but awaited orders. "Isolate the expedition data onto the secure analysis cluster in Lab Gamma. Full diagnostic quarantine before integration." He needed to keep this information contained until he understood the security of these systems.

As the team began the careful process, Volkov moved closer, peering at the initial raw data being triaged onto a display. "Absolutely fascinating waveforms, Dr. Thompson," he commented, his interest seeming genuine yet somehow predatory. "Extradimensional harmonics? Where did you manage to record such phenomena?"

Elijah chose his words carefully. "Derived from... private research, Doctor. Analysis of deep-field gravimetric distortions I've been pursuing since my... departure."

"Truly groundbreaking," Volkov murmured, his eyes scanning the data streams. "And the unique bio-signature referenced in the acquisition logs? Associated with these energy readings?"

Elijah felt Maya tense almost imperceptibly beside him. He needed a convincing reason for Eira's absence. "Ah, yes. The... subject exhibiting the resonance required immediate transfer to a specialized bio-containment facility off-world. Level Five protocols, given the unknown potential. Standard procedure for unique finds of this magnitude."

Volkov nodded slowly, still studying the data, though his eyes held a thoughtful, almost calculating glint. "Of course. Prudent. Keep me apprised of your analysis, Doctors." He smiled again, that smooth, unreadable expression, before turning back to the main console.

Elijah exchanged a quick, worried glance with Maya. They had bought themselves time, access. But they were operating blind in a facility – and perhaps a reality – that was no longer truly their own, under the watchful eye of a man whose position made no sense, and whose motives were terrifyingly unclear.

Silence pressed in on Eira from the unfamiliar walls of the Bramah chamber, but it wasn't truly silent inside her head. A low, persistent hum resonated behind her eyes, a phantom echo of the energy pulse that had ripped through the lab... through *them*. She sat curled on the resting platform, tracing the smooth, cool surface of the Keystone shard in her hand. *How?* The question pulsed with the hum. How could this tiny object be tied to such vast, terrifying power? Was the hum *from* the shard? Or the one Erebus held? Or the Prime Keystone itself, now an awakened, angry presence deep inside Vestara?

She closed her eyes, shutting out the alien room, and focused inward, pushing past the distracting hum, past the lingering fear. She pictured Erebus, recalling the brief, intense connection during the pulse. *Reach.* It felt like extending a hand into echoing darkness.

...Erebus...? Her thought felt small, tentative. *...Are you there...? That... sound... is it you?*

A pause stretched, filled only by the maddening hum. Then, a flicker, faint but definite.

Eira. Yes. His mental 'voice' felt strained, distant. *Gods, make it stop. The noise... it's not me. You have it too?*

Relief warred with dread. *Yes. Louder... since Lila...* She pictured the two shards nearing each other, the sudden, violent ripple. *...since the pulse. Is it these things? The shards?*

Or what they connect to. Erebus's thought felt heavy. *The power... it felt like the whole multiverse shuddered.* A shared wave of dizziness seemed to pass between them through the fragile link. *How can these small stones... hold that?*

I don't know. Eira clutched her shard tighter. *Mine... it let me hide. Vanish. I thought that was all.*

There was a sense of surprise from Erebus. *Hide? Mine... it lets me slip through things sometimes. Hear whispers.* A pause. *But nothing like... like that. They said reality changed out there because of this.* The thought was laced with cold fear.

Changed how? Eira desperately wanted to ask, but the fear was too strong. *They separated us. They have to keep these apart now. Until they understand.* A fragile hope surfaced. *These Bramah... they seem powerful. Careful. Surely they know how to control this?*

She felt Erebus's focus turn inward, perhaps examining his own shard, seeking answers in its silent depths. His response was slow, uncertain.

They have knowledge. Power. But this... this feels different. Older. A shared understanding flowed between them, stark and terrifying. *Whatever we're connected to... it's dangerous. And maybe... maybe we are too.*

The connection felt thin again, strained by the distance and the overwhelming implications. Eira opened her eyes, finding herself alone again in the quiet room, the hum a constant, unnerving reminder of the power she held, the peril Erebus had warned of, and the vast, frightening unknown they were now inextricably part of.

Aethon knelt at the base of the Cosmic Tree, the ambient light of the Starseed groves casting shifting, otherworldly patterns on the obsidian floor. He didn't just touch the Tree; he pressed his essence against its ancient consciousness, feeling the slow, steady pulse of innumerable realities branching from its roots. Weariness settled deep in his immortal bones, a fatigue born not of years, but of millennia witnessing the ebb and flow of cosmic tides – and the recent, jarring disruption he felt responsible for. He centered himself, quieting the anxious static left by the Keystone's chaotic activation, and focused his entire being, reaching out beyond the Tree, beyond the stronghold, towards the source of all balance.

"Father of Creation... Elyon... Hear Your servant... Grant guidance..." His prayer wasn't spoken aloud but resonated outwards, a wave of weary devotion seeking its anchor.

The air around him grew still, the gentle rustle of the Starseed leaves fading into a profound silence. The light didn't just brighten; it shifted, taking on impossible hues, coalescing into a presence *behind* and *around* him. It was a warmth like the heart of a newborn star, an age that dwarfed his own considerable lifespan, a peace that promised dissolution into perfect harmony. Elyon didn't step down; He simply *was*, His awareness enveloping Aethon like an ocean.

A voice, simultaneously vast as colliding galaxies and intimate as a heartbeat, resonated not in his ears, but in the core of his spirit. ***The weight you carry, My son. The echo of fractured balance. It troubles you deeply.***

Aethon didn't need to articulate his fear; he simply allowed the divine presence to perceive it – the image of timelines fraying, the memory of Lila's horrified expression, the gnawing question: *Have we, in our haste, broken Your creation, Father?*

The presence intensified, a feeling of gentle but absolute perspective washing over him. ***The multiverse bends, Aethon, but it does not so*** *easily break. The ripples from the Prime Keystone's stirring are but tremors. Existence endures this.*

A wave of relief washed through Aethon, so potent he slumped forward, his forehead pressing harder against the cool bark of the Tree, but the respite was immediately chased away by a profound sense of gravity, a shift in the divine focus that chilled him despite the overwhelming warmth.

Yet, a greater crucible approaches. A moment of convergence. A decision awaits, not of the Gods, but placed upon the fulcrum of existence itself. One choice, Aethon, upon which the fate of all realities will turn.

The immensity of it stole Aethon's breath. *How? Who? Such a burden... surely it falls to You, to the Elder Gods?*

The gentle pressure of Elyon's awareness seemed to steady him. *It is Our will that the choice be made within the tapestry We have woven. When the moment arrives, the path – though perhaps shrouded – will be discernible. Faith, Aethon. Trust in the balance, even when it seems lost. Trust that the right choice can be made.*

The weight of responsibility felt heavier now, not lighter. He bowed his head further, accepting the terrifying ambiguity, the profound burden. *"As You will, Father."*

The light softened, the colors receding back into the Tree's ethereal glow. The immense presence gently withdrew, like a receding tide, leaving behind a lingering resonance of peace mingled with the heavy weight of prophecy. Aethon remained kneeling for a long moment, utterly alone again in the quiet sanctum. The immediate crisis felt dwarfed by the looming unknown. *A decision... deciding the fate of all lives...* Whose decision? When? And how could any being, mortal or immortal, bear the weight of choosing correctly when the path itself was veiled? The comfort he sought had been replaced by a far more profound, and terrifying, sense of purpose.

Guardians of the Keystones: Echoes

C**hapter Eight**

A veil of swirling black mist, unnervingly silent, coalesced on the deserted landing platform high atop the Aurora Initiative tower. From its depths stepped Raven Locke and Nightshade, the sterile, recycled air of the facility tasting alien after the Void space of their transport. Nightshade murmured a final sibilant phrase, and the mist seemed to cling to them, deepening the ambient shadows around their forms, rendering them less substantial, harder to track. They slipped through the main doors like exhaled breaths.

Inside, the corridors were sleek, utilitarian, brightly lit – an environment hostile to their nature. Nightshade paused, head tilted, ignoring the hum of the building's systems. "The residue...her resonance," she whispered, the sound barely disturbing the air. "Strongest...this way. Upper levels."

Raven scanned ahead, noting the passive sensor arrays, the occasional security drone gliding silently past. "Their awareness is technological. Crude. But thorough. Stay within the deepest shadows."

They bypassed the main transport lifts, opting for a service conduit Nightshade opened with a gesture that made the nearby lights flicker almost imperceptibly. They ascended, emerging onto the residential level designated in the mission briefing.

The silence within Dr. Adrian Volkov's private laboratory was absolute, a carefully engineered void designed for pure, undiluted focus. Nestled deep within the command sector, it was his inner sanctum—a place of polished chrome, obsidian data-slates, and strange, inert artifacts displayed in vacuum-sealed cases, trophies from his own discreetly funded and highly classified off-world expeditions. He sat, not relaxed, but in a state of poised readiness, observing a multi-layered simulation of stellar nursery collapse on his primary holographic display.

A chime, soft and dissonant, broke the sterile quiet. It was a sound no one else in the entire Aurora Initiative would have recognized, an auditory flag tied to a monitoring system of his own clandestine design. Volkov's eyes, cold and analytical, shifted from the dying star on the main display to a small, isolated console to his left.

On it, a single, jagged waveform pulsed with a sickly violet light. It was not an equipment malfunction; the system diagnostics were green. It was not a radiation spike; the energy was heatless, massless. It was, by every metric of his secret research, a thaumic event. An incursion of forces that defied conventional physics.

His expression remained impassive, but his mind worked with cold, swift precision. He cross-referenced the locus of the event. Residential Level, Sector Gamma-7. An innocuous sector, mostly housing mid-level xeno botanists and their families. He brought up the personnel files for the area. Dr. Thompson and Dr. Singh's teams. The same people who had been involved with the Bramah and the Keystone. His eyes narrowed. A coincidence? He did not believe in them.

His fingers moved with practiced economy, tapping a hidden comm panel embedded beneath the cool surface of his desk. The connection was instantaneous, secure, and silent.

"Alpha team," Volkov's voice was a low, steady baritone, devoid of alarm but carrying an immense weight of authority. "Report."

A clipped, professional voice responded immediately in his private audio implant, a voice that belonged not to standard Aurora Security, but to his own hand-picked, private tactical team. *"Alpha is active and ready, Dr. Volkov."*

On his main display, the stellar nursery vanished, replaced by a detailed, multi-level schematic of Sector Gamma-7. He highlighted a specific residential block, the energy signature's ghost still shimmering there.

"I have a confirmed Class-Three thaumic incursion at these coordinates," he stated. "The signature is non-technological and deliberately shielded. This is not a drill."

"Understood, sir."

"I want a silent sweep protocol," Volkov commanded, his eyes tracing the labyrinthine corridors on the schematic, already calculating angles of approach and containment. "No overt engagement unless you are compromised. Your objective is intelligence. I want the source of this power identified. I want to know who is moving pieces on my board without my permission. Engage and report."

"Engaging now," was the immediate, final reply.

The connection closed. Adrian Volkov leaned back in his chair, his fingers steepling before him. His face was a mask of calm, analytical focus, but a cold, calculating fury settled deep within him. An unknown power had just made a move within his domain, targeting the very people connected to the greatest secret he was pursuing. He would unearth it, understand it, and then, he would control it or erase it.

Nightshade stopped before a nondescript door. "Here. The echoes are loudest." A wave of her hand, and the lock mechanism clicked open soundlessly. They slipped inside Eira's former quarters. The room was clinically clean, impersonal, scrubbed of physical traces. But the *energy*... it vibrated, thick with residual fear, confusion, and something else – a burgeoning power.

Raven immediately took up a position by the door, senses straining, listening to the distant sounds of the facility, while Nightshade moved to the center of the small room. Closing her eyes, Nightshade extended gaunt fingers, tracing unseen patterns in the air. Wisps of shadow flowed from her fingertips, coalescing, probing the lingering psychic impressions.

"Fear... intense," Nightshade murmured, her voice taking on a distant, echoing quality. "Confusion... meeting another... Singh... telepathic contact... strong... male presence..." Images flickered behind Nightshade's closed eyelids – disjointed, fragmentary. "...taken... powerful transport... shielded... guarded... warriors of light... the resonance... *Bramah!* She is with the Bramah!"

A faint clatter echoed from down the corridor. Raven tensed. "Movement," she hissed. "Multiple contacts. Coordinated."

Nightshade's brow furrowed, trying to grasp more – a location, a weakness – but the echoes were fading, disrupted perhaps by her own probing or the passage of time.

"They're coming closer," Raven warned, drawing a blade that seemed forged from frozen shadow. "Now, Nightshade!"

Nightshade's eyes snapped open, the ritual breaking abruptly. With a sharp, guttural word, she thrust her hands forward, tearing a ragged hole in the air before them – a swirling vortex of the same chaotic black mist that brought them here. Heavy footsteps pounded just outside the door.

"Go!" Raven urged, covering their retreat as Nightshade plunged into the portal. Raven followed an instant later, diving through as the door to the quarters burst inward.

Dr. Volkov swept into the room, flanked by his black-clad Alpha team guards, weapons raised. He scanned the empty space, his gaze immediately drawn to the far wall where the last tendrils of the unnatural mist were rapidly dissipating into nothingness. He felt the faint, acrid tang of Void energy, the residue of dark magic. A cold, calculating understanding settled on his face.

"Order of the Veil," he murmured, the name spoken with a chilling familiarity. He turned to his lead guard. "They know she was here. Full spectral analysis of this room. Initiate facility-wide countermeasures against thaumaturgic field manipulation and dimensional breaches, priority Alpha. I want this building bulletproofed against their *kind*."

The guard nodded curtly. Volkov lingered a moment longer, eyes narrowed in thought. The Order moving so quickly... they were more involved than he'd anticipated. This complicated matters. And potentially...created opportunities. He turned and strode out, already formulating new plans.

Back in the subtly altered Aurora Initiative lab, Dr. Volkov watched Elijah and Maya direct their team, his expression thoughtful, almost placid. He observed the careful isolation of the new data, the nervous energy of Thompson and Singh as they tried to reconcile the familiar environment with their jarring new reality. After several minutes of quiet observation, Volkov glanced discreetly at a small, encrypted datapad he carried. A minuscule light shifted from amber to green. His placid expression hardened slightly, replaced by a look of focused intent.

He approached the two doctors, interrupting their hushed, tense conversation about sensor discrepancies. "Doctors," his voice was smooth, betraying none of his inner thoughts, "continue your preliminary analysis. An urgent external matter requires my attention." He didn't offer details, didn't invite questions. "I anticipate returning within... three standard hours. Maintain current protocols."

Before Elijah or Maya could formulate more than a surprised acknowledgement, Volkov turned and strode purposefully towards the express lift, leaving them exchanging another look heavy with suspicion and unease. What "external matter" could be so urgent now?

Volkov bypassed the main docking bays. The lift descended to a sublevel, opening onto a private, dimly lit transit hub. A sleek, unmarked vessel, matte black and devoid of any Aurora Initiative insignia, waited silently. Volkov boarded without a word, and the craft detached, ascending not towards the sky, but angling down, skimming through the lower, less-monitored transit channels of Acarcis.

The journey was a stark contrast. The vessel left the gleaming, orderly sectors of the Initiative far behind, plunging into the decaying underbelly of the city – a district of crumbling infrastructure, flickering neon signs casting unreliable light on rain-slicked streets, and shadows that seemed unnaturally deep. The craft finally descended, not onto a platform, but into the cavernous, echoing space within a derelict hydro-plant, its landing lights briefly illuminating rusting turbines and graffiti-scarred walls.

Volkov disembarked into the damp, cool air. The entrance wasn't obvious – a section of reinforced wall slid aside silently as he approached. Inside, the aesthetic shifted again: minimalist, functional, dimly lit corridors of polished dark metal, silent save for the low hum of hidden systems. Security was invisible but palpable – subtle pressure changes underfoot, faint energy fields brushing against his clothes.

He walked directly towards a recessed alcove where a single figure sat before a bank of monitors displaying complex energy patterns and coded communication streams, their face obscured by shadow. The figure looked up, their eyes catching the minimal light.

"Sector Lead," the voice was quiet, neutral, devoid of inflection. "Your arrival is noted. The Archimandrite awaits you in the Sanctum."

Volkov gave a curt nod, his demeanor colder now, more disciplined than the persona he wore at Aurora. He proceeded down the long, sound-dampened corridor, passing several identical, heavily sealed doors. He reached the end, facing a single, imposing doorway crafted from the same dark, seamless metal. He paused for a fraction of a second, composing himself, before the door irised open at his proximity, granting him entry into the hidden heart of the Umbra Collective.

Aethon remained kneeling, the profound weight of Elyon's prophecy settling upon him, the silence of the Cosmic Tree's sanctum amplifying his troubled thoughts. He finally pushed himself slowly to his feet, the weariness not just in his limbs but in his very essence. As he gave the ancient Tree a final, reverent glance and turned to leave, the air before him shimmered, coalescing not with gentle warmth, but with the sharp, clear light of distant stars.

Nyx, Goddess of Wisdom, stood before him, her form precise, her eyes holding the vast, cool depth of cosmic knowledge. Aethon startled, stumbling back a step, the lingering peace of Elyon's presence instantly shattered by this new, unexpected manifestation. He bowed his head low, reverence mingling with sudden apprehension.

"Goddess Nyx! An unexpected..."

"There is no time for formality, Aethon," her voice cut through the air, clear and sharp as fractured crystal, devoid of preamble. "Events accelerate. A correction is required. Immediately."

Aethon straightened, sensing the profound urgency radiating from her. "Goddess?"

"Your order to separate the mortals – countermand it," Nyx stated, her gaze piercing, leaving no room for argument. "They must be brought into proximity once more. Their continued separation, after the resonance cascade, is causing a *different* instability. The Prime Keystone's matrix... it degrades without their balanced, proximal resonance."

Aethon felt a jolt, confusion warring with the fresh memory of the chaos unleashed. "But, Goddess... bringing them together... the activation..."

"Physical contact," Nyx clarified, her tone leaving no doubt. "Either between the shards themselves, or the mortal hosts. *That* is the trigger for the chaotic release. Absolute separation, however, starves the matrix. It unravels." She leaned forward slightly, the starlight in her eyes seeming to intensify. "Think of it as a stabilizing orbit, Aethon. Too close, they collide with catastrophic results. Too distant, the gravitational bond fails, and the system collapses. They must be near, yet distinct. Hurry. The degradation accelerates with every moment they remain apart."

The impossible nature of the situation struck Aethon – damned if they touch, damned if they're separated. A razor's edge. He swallowed, the weight of responsibility heavier than ever. "I... understand, Goddess. Your will be done."

Nyx gave a single, sharp nod, her form dissolving back into shimmering motes of light that faded into the ambient glow of the Tree. Aethon didn't pause. He spun, already moving towards the exit, his weariness burned away by adrenaline and divine imperative. He activated his internal comms, his voice ringing with clipped authority.

"Lila! Prepare Lab Prime for subject observation! Guards, retrieve subjects Eira and Erebus *now*. Escort to Lab Prime, separate entrances. Maintain minimum five meters distance between them *at all times*. Confirm!"

He raced through the stronghold corridors, arriving at the laboratory just as the guards were escorting a confused Eira through one door and a wary Erebus through another, keeping them carefully positioned on opposite sides of the large chamber. Lila looked up from her console, her face paling as she saw them both.

"Aethon!" she exclaimed, rising quickly. "Bringing them together again? Is this wise? After the readings..."

"Nyx commands it," Aethon cut her off, his voice firm, overriding her valid scientific concerns with the weight of divine mandate. He gestured towards the energy readings still fluctuating uneasily on the main screen. "Separation unravels the Keystone, Lila. Proximity stabilizes it – *if* they remain apart. No contact. Monitor every energy fluctuation, every resonance shift. We are balanced on a precipice."

He stood between the two mortals, a guardian enforcing a dangerous, necessary proximity, the tension in the lab thick enough to taste, acutely aware that the fate of the multiverse might hinge on preventing a single, accidental touch.

The air in the Order of the Veil's hidden shrine was thick and stagnant, tasting of decay and stale fear. Nightshade knelt at the center of a complex sigil etched onto the cold stone floor in what looked disturbingly like dried blood mixed with powdered bone. Flickering candles, rendered from substances best left unnamed, cast greasy, undulating shadows that seemed to writhe independently of the weak flames. Her eyes, voids in her pale face, darted around the oppressive chamber, drawing unseen threads of dark energy towards the sigil's heart. She chanted in a low, guttural language that scraped against the silence, her own form flickering slightly, as if struggling to maintain cohesion while channeling the required power.

Slowly, a point above the sigil began to shimmer, not with light, but with an oily, light-devouring darkness. It coalesced into a churning vortex, pulling warmth from the air, the temperature in the shrine dropping noticeably. Within this vortex, an image resolved – distorted, unstable, like a reflection on disturbed water – the sharp, cruel features of a Shivara female, her eyes burning with the cold, merciless fire of the Void.

Lord Valerius, who had been watching with hungry intensity from the shadows just beyond the sigil's edge, stepped forward, bowing low but unable to entirely mask the ambitious gleam in his eyes.

The image in the vortex spoke, her voice layered, like shifting ice overlaying whispers from a tomb. **"Valerius. You disturb the Master's preparations. This intrusion carries a cost. Speak."** There was no greeting, only cold demand.

"Magnificent Niamh," Valerius began, his voice an oily blend of subservience and eagerness. "We offer intelligence. Confirmation, perhaps, of value to the glorious Shivara... to Master Kael's hunt."

The image shimmered, Niamh's lip curling slightly in disdain. **"We are aware of the Bramah's quarry. What *value* can the Order offer beyond failure?"** The unspoken reference to Raven and Nightshade's recent retreat from Aurora HQ hung in the frigid air.

Valerius's smile didn't waver, though a flicker of resentment crossed his eyes. "We confirm the mortal is the *female* they sought. Resonant with Keystone power. Potentially... a wielder." He paused, choosing his words carefully. "Direct infiltration of the Bramah stronghold proved... challenging. Their wards are potent. However," he leaned forward conspiratorially, "our agents *did* ascertain the mortal was processed by the Aurora Initiative on Solara prior to Bramah extraction. That Initiative possesses detailed scans, energy profiles... data the Bramah might lack. Data that could perhaps be... acquired."

Niamh's burning eyes seemed to consider this, the vortex pulsing slightly. **"Aurora Initiative data... yes. Potentially useful ancillary information. Acquire it. Covertly this time, Valerius. Do not draw unnecessary attention."** Her voice was dismissive. **"Kael will focus on retrieving the asset directly from the Bramah. Do not interfere."**

Before Valerius could offer further assurances, the connection snapped. The vortex imploded, plunging the shrine into near total darkness, leaving only the greasy candlelight and a lingering, bone-deep chill.

Valerius slowly straightened, the subservient mask falling away, replaced by a cold, calculating smile that didn't reach his eyes. He turned to Raven Locke, who had materialized silently from the shadows behind him.

"The Shivara underestimate us," Valerius murmured, more to himself than to her. "They see us as tools." He looked at Raven. "Secure the Aurora data, Raven. All of it. Let the Shivara hunt the Bramah. We will gather our *own* understanding of this power." His smile widened, filled with dark ambition. The Order of the Veil served the Dark Gods, yes, but Valerius served his own ascent first and foremost.

The biting wind whipped around Raven Locke as she crouched on the precipice of a neighboring skyscraper, gazing across the gulf at the monolithic Aurora Initiative tower. Nightshade's rituals were blocked – Volkov, whoever he was, had been thorough. But technology and shadow remained her allies. A near-invisible micro-grapple line shot across the gap, anchoring silently. Taking a deep breath, she launched herself into the abyss, trusting her augmented reflexes and the stealth suit that drank the ambient light.

She bypassed the main landing platform, accessing a rarely used maintenance conduit several levels down – a blind spot even Volkov's recent upgrades seemed to have missed. Inside, the air was cold, metallic. She moved with liquid grace, her boots making no sound, her form melting into the deeper pools of shadow cast by humming machinery. She bypassed pressure plates, navigated flickering laser grids tied into new energy dampers, her senses alert for the faintest electronic whisper of detection.

But Volkov was waiting. Not physically, but electronically. As Raven accessed a junction box to tap into the internal network directories, bypassing standard security protocols with practiced ease, a silent flag tripped deep within Volkov's private command suite. On his console, a schematic highlighted her point of entry and predicted trajectory. *Anomalous Network Access: Maintenance Conduit 7B. Non-Standard Bypass.* A cold smile touched Volkov's lips. He watched her icon move on his display towards the central data archives. *Predictable.* He let her proceed, issuing quiet commands to his Alpha team via neural link.

Raven reached the data archive – a vault-like room, colder than the corridors. She bypassed the formidable lock, slipping inside. Rows upon rows of servers hummed softly. She moved to a primary terminal, her fingers flying across the interface, slicing through layers of standard Aurora encryption. She targeted files related to the Vestara expedition, energy signatures matching Eira's known resonance, cross-referencing with known Keystone frequencies pulled from Order databases. Partial scans, fragmented analysis, Elijah Thompson's preliminary notes... useful, but incomplete. Where was the core data? Was Volkov hiding it elsewhere?

Suddenly, the heavy archive door hissed shut behind her, locking with a series of resounding *thuds*. Red emergency lights flooded the room, casting everything in a bloody glow. Simultaneously, a low, penetrating hum filled the air, pressing in on her senses – an energy field designed to disrupt more than just technology. She instinctively reached out, mentally or perhaps for a hidden device, to contact Nightshade – nothing. Only static, a suffocating deadness where the connection should have been. Trapped.

A section of the far wall slid open, revealing Dr. Volkov, flanked by two imposing guards in black, weaponized armor, their faces hidden behind reflective visors. Volkov stepped forward, his hands clasped behind his back, an unnerving calm on his face. He even allowed himself a small, dry chuckle.

"Looking for something, Ms. Locke?"

Raven spun, instinctively dropping into a low crouch, her shadow-forged blade appearing in her hand as if by magic – one trick the dampeners couldn't fully negate. "How do you know my name?" she hissed, her eyes darting around, assessing angles, calculating odds she already knew were impossible.

"Facial recognition is remarkably efficient," Volkov replied smoothly, ignoring her blade. "As are the countermeasures I implemented after your colleague's rather... unsubtle visit. Thaumic energy dampeners. Network intrusion alerts tuned to non-standard signatures. Your magic, your escape routes... quite useless in here. You were detected the moment you bypassed the first security layer."

"Trapping me gains you nothing, *worm*," Raven spat, channeling controlled fury. "The Order will know."

"Oh, I'm counting on it," Volkov said, his smile widening slightly. "Because while killing you would be simple, it's rather unproductive. I have a proposal for your masters. An offer I believe they, and perhaps even the entities they whisper to, will find... compelling."

Raven narrowed her eyes, suspicion warring with a flicker of pragmatic curiosity. "The likes of *you*... offering something to the Order? To the *Shivara*? Your petty science is nothing."

"My science," Volkov corrected calmly, gesturing around the humming archive, "is rapidly evolving. We possess data – detailed scans, resonance profiles of the Keystone energy, analysis of the... subject... you seek. Information your Order failed to acquire. Information I am willing to trade."

"For what price?" Raven asked, keeping her blade steady.

Volkov's eyes glittered with ambition. "Access. An introduction. Not for me, personally, nor for this... Initiative." He paused, letting the name hang in the air. "For the **Umbra Collective**. We seek dialogue. With those who command the shadows your Order serves. A simple introduction, facilitated by you, is the first step."

Raven stared, processing the implications. Umbra Collective? This man wasn't just an ambitious scientist; he represented another player entirely, one with significant resources and disturbing knowledge. She was trapped, her mission a failure, but this... this was unexpected intelligence.

"Release me," Raven said, her voice cold and level. "And I will convey your message to Lord Valerius. He will decide if your... Collective... warrants the attention of our patrons. No guarantees."

"That is all I require for now, Ms. Locke," Volkov nodded, seemingly satisfied. "A message delivered. But impress upon your superiors: this door opens only once. The Umbra Collective holds keys your masters may find surprisingly valuable." He gestured to the guards. "Escort Ms. Locke out. Secure bypass corridor Delta. Ensure she leaves... unobserved."

The guards moved forward, weapons still raised, as Volkov turned away, already accessing his console, his mind clearly moving onto the next phase of his intricate game. Raven, disarmed and flanked, allowed herself to be led away, her mind racing, analyzing this new, dangerous player who dared bargain with the shadows.

Guardians of the Keystones: Echoes

Chapter Nine

The sudden quiet from the sensors was almost more jarring than their earlier, frantic shrieking. Aethon let out a breath he hadn't realized he'd been holding, a shallow, unsteady thing. The hum was steady now, yes, but it felt thin, like ice stretched over a churning abyss. Any moment, it could crack.

Lila's face, pale and strained in the flickering emergency lumens of the monitoring chamber, was turned towards him. Her eyes, wide and dark, searched his, a silent, desperate plea for an explanation that could make sense of the volatile energies they had barely, just barely, contained. The tremor in her hands as she clutched a data slate betrayed the fear she clearly fought to control.

Aethon forced his face into a mask of command, though the knot in his stomach tightened. "It's... stable," he managed, his voice tighter than he intended. "For now. The mortals—" his gaze flickered towards the shielded observation window, beyond which nothing could be truly seen, only inferred, "—they *must* remain in close proximity. It seems the Prime Keystone... its influence is volatile, and it *demands* this configuration." The last words felt heavy, forced out against a rising tide of unease.

"But the Goddess..." Lila's voice was a whisper, almost lost in the thrum of the now-subdued machinery. "Her pronouncement? Why like this? Why *now*?" The unspoken 'what have we gotten ourselves into?' hung thick between them.

Aethon's jaw clenched. "She *ordered* it." The finality in his tone was meant to quell, but it only amplified the oppressive uncertainty. "That is all that is required of us to understand." He left unsaid, *And perhaps all we are capable of understanding.*

"Yes, Commander." Lila's assent was barely audible, her gaze dropping to the flickering readings on her slate, as if seeking solace in data that offered none. "By the Gods... it will be done." She swallowed, the sound stark in the tense silence. What 'it' truly meant, and what new horrors this precarious balance held at bay—or worse, might unleash—was a cold dread coiling in her heart.

Meanwhile, within the unseen, heavily warded containment chamber at the heart of the facility, Eira's senses swam. The oppressive, chaotic static that had threatened to tear her mind apart had receded, leaving behind a throbbing, electric stillness. She looked towards Erebus, her only anchor in this terrifying new reality, hoping his stoic exterior hid some clue, some understanding she lacked. She reached out, a tendril of thought, fragile and uncertain.

"Erebus... do you... do you understand any of this?"

His mental touch was a raw nerve, frayed and stretched taut. *"I think... the Shards within us... they need to be near. The chaos outside... can you feel it? It lessens when we are... close."* His thought carried the bitter taste of something deeply unnatural.

Relief, sharp and desperate, pierced through Eira's fear. *"Yes! I can feel mine... it's humming now. Almost... singing. A strange, high vibration. It's not tearing at me anymore. Do you feel that too? Is yours... calm?"*

A wave of pure, undiluted cold washed back from him, extinguishing her brief flicker of hope. *"Singing? Mine feels no song, Eira. It feels... rage. A contained inferno. This proximity, it's like a chain pulled too tight.*

It wants to lash out, to shatter. It's not singing. It's screaming to be free of this."

From the empyrean heart of Elysium, where timeless light bathes the sanctuary of the Elder Gods, a Voice of pure resonance emanated. It was Elyon, from whom creation's first breath, harmony's first chord, and peace's deepest sigh flowed.

"Illumination," His thought echoed through the hallowed expanse, **"must We now impart unto the Bramah, Our devoted children."**

A presence, measured as the march of ages and structured as the cosmos itself, manifested. Kronos, the Weaver of Time, Shepherd of Order, drew nearer, his essence a steady cadence in the eternal stillness.

"Yet, Father Elyon," Kronos's voice was the sound of ages turning, **"the Prime Keystone remains veiled, its sacred heart hidden from Our pervasive gaze."**

Elyon's divine consciousness pulsed with a profound query. **"A paradox unfolds. All threads of existence lie bare before Us, from the first star's whisper to the last echo of being. Yet this Keystone... this anchor of realities... conceals its very soul from its makers. Was it not by Our divine will, through these very conduits, that We wove the tapestry of creation in the dawn of time?"**

Kronos responded, his tone resonating with the immutable laws he embodied, **"Through endless cycles, Great Architect, the true nature of the Keystones has ever been a sacred enigma, their deepest truths beyond even Our complete knowing. Such is the ordained pattern, woven into the fabric of eternity itself since their inception."**

A shimmer of divine concern flowed from Elyon. **"Then how shall Our light guide the Bramah in this, if We Ourselves perceive only** shadows around this core mystery? **A path to its heart *must* be found. Its veiled truths *must* be unveiled unto Us, for the sake of all that We have wrought."**

"**Even so.**" Kronos's voice gained a resonant certainty, like the final click of a cosmic lock falling into place. **"A conduit to its core *shall* be opened. Through the currents of time and the unwavering principles of order, a way will be made manifest. I shall devote My being to this revelation."**

And with that vow, the presence of Kronos receded, like the tide of a celestial ocean returning to its unfathomable depths, leaving Elyon to ponder within the boundless silence and radiant light of His divine contemplation.

Aethon paced the command deck, the star-strewn void beyond the main viewport a dizzying, indifferent canvas to their immediate crisis. He barely registered Thorne's swift, silent approach, his mind already grappling with a dozen impossible scenarios. The air crackled with unspoken tension.

Thorne's voice was clipped, cutting straight to the point. "Any further clarity on the directive, Commander? Anything at all?"

Aethon's response was a bitten-off growl, his frustration palpable. "Precious little, Thorne! It's a hornet's nest of questions and damn few answers. We're operating blind."

"So, our next move?" Thorne didn't waste a breath. "The Prime Keystone? Direct readings might give us *something* tangible, something to act on before it's too late."

Aethon slammed a fist onto the cool metal of the nearest console, the impact a dull thud in the otherwise humming room. "It's our only viable option, and the clock is ticking! Yes! Mobilize your best team. Take Lila – her expertise is non-negotiable for this. Get those extended readings from the Keystone." He leaned in, his voice dropping to a steely intensity. "And Thorne – *speed* is paramount. Every moment we hesitate, the Shivara gain ground. We *must* not let them get there first, or even suspect our play."

"Understood, Commander." Thorne's affirmation was sharp, immediate. "We move now."

He was already turning, a blur of motion heading for the exit, gone before the words fully settled. Aethon was left alone, staring out at the cold, swirling galaxies, the chilling awareness of the Shivara's pursuit a tightening vise around his thoughts. Time was a luxury they no longer possessed.

Thorne was barely out the command deck door, his mind already on team assembly, when Lila's voice, tight with an almost unbearable tension, crackled over the comms, overriding all channels: *"Commander Aethon, Thorne—return to my lab! Now! It's... it's critical!"*

The air in Lila's lab was frigid despite the hum of equipment, a stark contrast to the frantic energy radiating from the scientist herself. They found her white-faced before her main display, hands trembling as she gestured towards a complex, rapidly shifting energy schematic that pulsed with an ominous light.

"Commander," she breathed, her usual composure utterly shattered, her voice strained. "The data... it's undeniable. The energies within the mortals—Eira and Erebus—they're not two separate Shard-traces as we presumed. They're... they're polarizing aspects of a *singular* Shard, Commander! And this Shard..." Her voice cracked, a tremor of horrified awe in her eyes. "By all the Gods, it's the *Heart* of the Prime Keystone itself! Its core, its active regulator!"

Aethon stared, the star-chilled vastness he'd just been observing seeming to rush into the room, suffocating him. The color drained from his own face. "The *Heart*?" His voice was a rasp. "How is that even conceivable? What in the name of the First Light does that *mean* for us, for *them*?" The questions were sharp, each one laced with a dawning, sickening horror. The weight of the Goddess's recent, inscrutable order regarding their proximity pressed down on him with new, terrifying significance.

Lila shook her head, her gaze fixed on the alarming display, her earlier anxiousness now morphing into a profound dread. "It means the Prime Keystone isn't just an ancient artifact, Commander. It's... it may be sentient. Possess a will." She gestured vaguely towards where Eira and Erebus were held, her hand unsteady. "And those mortals... they weren't just *found* by chance, nor were they mere vessels. The Keystone *chose* them. There's something intrinsic to their nature, something it specifically requires, something it's now actively drawing upon. This isn't random; it's a design unfolding, a purpose far greater, and potentially far more calamitous, than we ever imagined."

A living Keystone? Chosen mortals? A plan? Aethon's mind reeled, the foundations of their understanding cracking beneath him. The questions hammered at him, each more terrifying than the last. What did this ancient, aware entity *want*? What would it do to Eira and Erebus to achieve its unfathomable ends? He felt the abyss open, the chilling weight of that unknown consciousness pressing in, demanding... something. And the Shivara—that relentless, shadowy threat—they were still out there, a closing vise. There was no time for careful deliberation, no room for error, only for desperate, immediate action.

He whirled on Thorne, his voice a raw command that cut through the charged atmosphere. "Thorne! Your mission parameters have changed—radically! Get to the Prime Keystone! The readings are secondary now, almost an afterthought! Your priority: *attempt to establish communication*, if such a thing is even possible with a... a living Keystone! Find out what it is, what it wants with them, with *us*! But be ready for anything—*anything*! Go! Now! Every second is a drop of blood we cannot afford to lose!"

The oppressive silence of their confinement pressed in. Eira, seeking an anchor beyond the unsettling hum of her own inner resonance, reached out with a delicate tendril of thought, a whisper in the shared space of their minds.

"Erebus... are you... can you sense me? I need to understand... something."

His mental presence answered, not with warmth, but with a weary acknowledgment, like old stone shifting. *"I'm here, Eira. The Shards, isn't it? Why yours feels like... music, and mine is a caged beast."*

A wave of relief, tinged with her persistent anxiety, flowed from her. *"Yes. Exactly. Why would one sing, while the other only knows... rage?"*

There was a pause, a drawing inward, then his thoughts began to unspool, not as words alone, but as echoes of sensations, bleak and sharp. *"Perhaps it's not the Shard alone... but what it found. Or what found it."*

He let her glimpse it then—Asphodel. Not a story, but the raw *feel* of it: the acrid bite of chemical winds, the perpetual twilight under a sky scarred by ancient cosmic fallout, the grinding desolation of an industrial graveyard. She saw, through his mind's eye, colossal, rusting mega-structures clawing at the toxic sky like skeletal fingers, slag fields stretching into metallic deserts, and the desperate, feral glimmer of scavenged settlements clinging to life within the ruins. The daily thrum of fear, the gnawing hunger, the icy touch of betrayal—it was a world where survival was a bloodied-knuckle fight, day after brutal day.

"I don't remember much before that," his thoughts continued, flat and cold. *"Orphaned young. You learned fast. Hesitate, you starve. Trust anyone... you die. Simple rules."*

Then, a flicker of something different amidst the bleakness: the ruin of a research outpost, ancient, forgotten. And there, a shard of crystal, cool against his desperate skin, yet thrumming with a life that Asphodel itself had long choked out. *"It was... different. It chose me, I think. A secret. Mine."*

The power had been erratic, a wild thing. He shared fleeting impressions: the dizzying slip through a corroded wall to evade a ganger's blade; the way shadows would deepen around him, swallowing him whole from a patrol's searching eyes; the sudden, jarring premonition of hostile intent moments before an ambush. Not control. Just... survival, the Shard an extension of his will to live.

And then, a new presence flickered in the shared memories—older, sharper, radiating a weary cynicism. *"Kaelen,"* Erebus's thought named him. *"A Shivara. Stranded there for centuries, he said. A ghost in the rust, like me, but... colder."* Kaelen, the ancient warrior, hadn't offered solace. He'd seen the Shard's energy, the boy's desperate, raw power, and perhaps found a grim utility, or a flicker of cruel amusement. The lessons were Shivara lessons: the brutal efficiency of a killing blow, the paranoia of constant vigilance, the cold calculus that power was the only truth, empathy a fatal flaw. Kaelen had honed Erebus's raw phasing, his cloaking in shadow, not as gifts, but as tools—to dominate, to survive, to *take*. Theirs was a mentorship of shared desolation, lasting years, until Kaelen finally clawed his way off that dying world.

The harsh impressions receded, leaving Eira shaken. Erebus's mental voice returned, touched with a grim finality. *"So, you see. Perhaps the Shard... it remembers. It reflects the world that cradled it. The life it clung to."*

A profound sorrow welled in Eira. *"Oh, Erebus... I'm so sorry. Your life... it was so cruel."* A softer, more luminous memory touched his mind—a fleeting image from her own past, tinged with light, a moment of fragile joy. *"Mine wasn't always easy, but there were... glimpses. Moments I could hold onto."*

Guardians of the Keystones: Echoes

Chapter Ten

The oppressive chill of the Order of the Veil's sanctum seeped into Raven Locke's bones, a familiar cold that did little to soothe the black fury still coiling in her gut. Above, the mundane world might exist, but here, beneath lightless vaults and weeping stone, only shadows thrived. Her return was not triumphant, but a grim procession through corridors that felt like the gullet of some slumbering beast. Adrian Volkov. The name was a brand, his capture of her a festering wound to her pride. *How could that mongrel, that upstart, have ensnared her so easily?*

The thought was a shard of glass, twisting. This "invitation" she carried for Lord Valerius had to be spun, transformed from the ashes of her humiliation into a calculated offering, lest the punishment awaiting her prove far more lingering than Volkov's fleeting victory. As she approached the final, obsidian-veined archway leading to Lord Valerius's sanctum, she forced a mask of cold composure over the inferno within, her breath steadying against the crushing weight of his anticipated judgment.

She stepped into the oppressive gloom. Lord Valerius was a deeper shadow upon shadows, his presence a palpable vortex that seemed to draw all warmth, all light, into itself.

"My Lord," Raven's voice was a low, carefully controlled tremor, barely disturbing the sepulchral air. "I return. With... intelligence. And an invitation, of a sort."

The air grew colder. Valerius's voice, when it came, was like the dry rustle of ancient parchment over bone. "Speak, Raven. What morsels of insight have you clawed from the darkness for us? And this... *invitation*? Do not tell me that one such as you allowed herself to be... *taken*." The word dripped with a chilling disdain.

A sliver of ice touched Raven's heart. "My Lord, his defenses... they were beyond anticipation. My arts, even the Veil's deeper blessings, were... stifled. As if smothered by an unknown, nullifying force."

"Failure, child, carves its own bleak rewards here," Valerius's voice was devoid of any inflection, making the threat more profound. "You had best possess something of true worth to offset this... lapse. What have you learned to justify this intrusion upon my contemplation?"

"They have unearthed a relic, my Lord," Raven kept her gaze downcast. "A 'Keystone,' they call it. Primordial. Impossibly powerful. And they know much – its location, deep within a neighboring system, its... nature."

A subtle shift in the shadows around Valerius, like a predator scenting blood. "A Keystone, you say?" The words were almost a caress. "Power of that magnitude... such a thing could draw the gaze of the Dark Gods themselves. This... this could be the offering that finally elevates us, that shows Them our unwavering devotion, our *true* value. We must possess this knowledge, Raven. At any cost."

"Yes, my Lord. But the cost is... specific." Raven hesitated, the words feeling like poison on her tongue. "The one who holds this knowledge, Adrian Volkov, he offers it... in exchange for an audience. With the Shivara. Or perhaps," her voice dropped further, "with the Dark Gods directly."

A pause, so profound it felt like the world held its breath.

"But he does not serve the Aurora Initiative, as our earlier whispers suggested," Raven continued, pressing on before Valerius could speak.

"He claims allegiance to another power, one unknown to our archives: the 'Umbra Collective.'"

"The Umbra Collective?" Valerius's voice was a silken hiss, laced with a sudden, sharp interest that was far more terrifying than open anger. "Another clot of shadow dwellers vying for scraps in the dark? We must unmake this Collective, peel back its secrets. No upstart cur will stand between the Order and the favor of the Gods. That would be... blasphemy." A chilling amusement touched his tone. "But perhaps this Volkov has a use yet. Present him to the Shivara, you say? A blood bounty. A willing sacrifice to sweeten our own petition for an audience. Ingenious, in its own crude way. Bring this fool, this Adrian Volkov, before me."

"It will be done, my Lord." The words were ash in Raven's mouth.

She bowed, a low, subservient gesture that belied the cold knot of apprehension tightening within her. As she retreated from the suffocating presence of Lord Valerius, his final command echoed in the darkness of her mind. Her next challenge: lure Volkov into this web of shadows. And deeper still, she knew, lay the imperative to exhume the motives of this Umbra Collective. In the intricate, deadly dance of shadows, a new, unknown player was a threat that could unravel everything.

Failure was a specter Raven Locke dared not entertain. Snaring Adrian Volkov would be child's play, a mere trifle. But the Umbra Collective... their secrets were cancers, buried deep within the city's marrow, a near-suicidal excavation for any who dared try. Yet, Raven's gaze fixed upon a single, fragile thread: Nalini Sharma. A Civic Data Archivist, a paper-pusher from Acarcis city center, unwittingly held the potential to unearth the festering truths Lord Valerius craved. Nalini, a lamb to be led to a slaughter of secrets.

Raven recalled with a predator's focus that Nalini clung to a pathetic dream: a pilgrimage to Solara's Crystal Canyon, scraping together meager credits. Such desires were levers, easily exploited. A quick, guttural command to Nightshade in the oppressive gloom of her quarters, and a whispered incantation rippled through the ether. The city's fabric warped, spitting Raven out near her unsuspecting prey. The city center's façade of order offered no sanctuary. Raven stalked Nalini to the maw of a stinking, unlit alley. In a heartbeat, she was on her – a phantom's embrace, cold steel kissing the archivist's tender throat.

Raven's voice, a silken rasp against the alley's grime, coiled around Nalini. "Information. There's a rot in this city, a shadow cabal. You will unearth it for me." The glint of the blade against Nalini's skin underscored the unspoken. "Your little pilgrimage? Consider the credits yours."

Nalini's breath hitched, a trapped bird. "Maybe... It depends how deeply it's buried."

"The Umbra Collective," Raven hissed, the name itself a venomous secret. "Dig it out. Bring it here. And breathe a word of this to another soul, your life is forfeit. Your secrecy is your only shield."

A choked, barely audible, "Understood."

Raven released her grip, a predator letting its mauled prey scuttle free. Nalini stumbled from the alley's darkness, her hurried steps echoing with a terror that would now be her constant companion as she fled towards the cold, indifferent archives of the city center.

The city archives offered Nalini nothing but digital ghosts. Hours bled into a nerve-wracking eternity as every search for the "Umbra Collective" returned a blank, echoing void. But as her fingers danced across the terminal, a chilling pattern began to emerge not from what was there, but what was *missing*. Entire swathes of data concerning certain influential organizations were meticulously redacted, their digital footprints erased with an efficiency that spoke of immense, unseen power. It was like staring at the outline of a predator, invisible but for the space it violently occupied.

A cold dread coiled in Nalini's stomach. The woman from the alley, with her blade and her chilling demands, was not someone to disappoint. The weight of that unspoken threat pressed down on her, making her dream of the Crystal Canyon feel like a fragile thing, easily shattered. Was this desperate gamble, this pact with the shadows, truly the only path to her pilgrimage? Each redacted file felt like a fresh wave of doubt, a silent accusation.

Her mind, a maelstrom of fear and fractured hopes, sifted through the digital detritus. File after corrupted file, screen after empty screen. Then, a flicker. A connection, almost too faint to grasp, began to thread itself through the corrupted data. As she leaned closer, her breath catching in her throat, the sterile glow of the terminal seemed to warp. The air grew heavy.

It wasn't a thought, not an inference. It was a deluge.

The world behind her eyelids fractured. One moment she was in the hushed archives, the next, the city outside was an alien landscape, subtly yet profoundly changed. Faces she thought she knew were distorted masks; familiar streets twisted into new, unsettling configurations. A silent, seismic shift had remade her reality, and she was the sole, horrified witness. No— a prickle of awareness, sharp and terrifying—there were others. Two more, their forms indistinct, yet she knew, with a certainty that defied logic, that they too saw. They were... altered, touched by some colossal, unseen entity. The vision offered no more, only the chilling certainty of their shared, secret sight.

Then came the names, a torrent of forbidden images and understanding. The Aurora Initiative, a gleaming façade hiding unknown depths. The Umbra Collective, a palpable darkness. Adrian Volkov, his face a shifting, untrustworthy blur, a man of two irreconcilable natures. The Order of the Veil, shrouded and ancient. And behind them, through them, *above* them, pulsed a power so vast, so terrifyingly indifferent, it dwarfed her comprehension.

The vision shattered, leaving her gasping, hands gripping the terminal, the ordinary hum of the archives roaring in her ears. Her heart hammered against her ribs. Was this real? Or had the strain, the fear, finally unhinged her mind? Yet, beneath the terror, a horrifying clarity settled. Her eyes, for the first time, had been forced open to a truth more dangerous than she could ever have imagined.

Thorne strode into Lila's lab, his steps quick with purpose, an almost palpable energy preceding him. Lila, already anticipating, looked up from a cascade of data streaming across her main terminal, her own focus sharpening.

"Lila," he began, his voice resonating with a new, vibrant edge, "the time has come. Can we prepare the mortals? They accompany us to Elyria—to the Keystone shrine itself!"

"To Elyria!" Lila's eyes widened almost imperceptibly, a spark of intense scientific thrill igniting within her usual calm, a thrill she quickly masked with professionalism. "Yes, Commander. Their proximity can be managed. No direct physical contact, of course—the consequences are... potent, and still largely unknown. But I can fine-tune the field dampeners and establish a direct, continuous monitor on the Prime Keystone's resonance from here. We *must* witness this phenomenon at its source!"

"Excellent!" Thorne's response was crisp. "Make them ready. We depart with the advance team—immediately!"

"Understood, Commander!" Lila was already turning to the comms for Eira and Erebus's shielded enclosure, her voice imbued with a newfound, carefully controlled eagerness. "Eira, Erebus! Prepare yourselves! We are embarking on a journey to Elyria, to the very heart of the energies you carry! A critical precaution: physical contact between you remains strictly forbidden. The energies involved... they demand precise orchestration for everyone's safety."

From within their separate observation fields, Eira and Erebus both gave a solemn nod of understanding, though a flicker of nervous anticipation, perhaps even hope, could be seen in their eyes. The air on the ship soon crackled with focused activity. Equipment was stowed with practiced speed, engines hummed to vibrant life, and their vessel seamlessly joined the waiting fleet. With a breathtaking surge that pressed them into their seats, the interstellar drive engaged, and in what felt like mere heartbeats, the vibrant, swirling clouds of the planet Vestara filled the main viewscreen, magnificent and beckoning.

"Transport sequence initiating!" Thorne announced over the ship-wide comm, his voice ringing with the thrill of imminent discovery. "To the Keystone shrine beneath Elyria! All teams, prepare for immediate disembarkation!"

The moment they materialized, the air in the Keystone shrine beneath Elyria thrummed, thick and electric with an ancient, resonant power that vibrated deep in their bones. It was a place of immense, contained energy, awe-inspiring and potent beyond measure, the very stones glowing with intricate, dormant patterns.

Instantly, Eira gasped, her head tilting as if listening to a distant, beautiful song. A wide, incredulous smile touched her lips. She reached out mentally to Erebus, her thoughts shimmering with excitement.

"Erebus! The humming... it's so clear here! So incredibly strong! Can you feel it too?"

Even Erebus, usually a bastion of stoicism, gave a curt nod, his gaze sweeping the monumental chamber, a flicker of something akin to profound wonder in his eyes. *"I hear it. It's... everywhere. Pulsating."*

The ambient hum in the shrine intensified, visibly causing dust motes to dance in the faint light filtering from fissures above. Its pitch climbed, shifting through octaves, becoming not just a sound but a palpable wave of energy that resonated within their very cells, harmonizing, focusing. Then, impossibly, miraculously, the unified humming coalesced, sharpening into something more, into—

"I LIVE."

A Voice, ancient beyond measure, clear as starlight, yet powerful as a nova, bloomed not in their ears, but directly within their minds, thrumming through every fiber of their being, a declaration that shook them to their core.

"I FEEL ALL."

Eira whirled towards Thorne, her eyes shining, alight with an almost unbearable, joyous excitement. "Commander!" Her voice was breathless, triumphant. "It spoke! The Keystone—it spoke to us again!"

Thorne leaned forward, his own expression taut with barely suppressed elation, his hand gripping the hilt of his sidearm as if to steady himself against the momentousness of the event. "What, Eira? What did it say?! Tell us!"

Eira's voice was a beacon of wonder in the resonating chamber. "It said: *I live. I feel all!*"

Thorne, still reeling from the Keystone's electrifying declaration, snapped into action, his voice sharp with a new, fervent energy that resonated through the ancient shrine. "Lila! Begin full spectrum analysis! Focus on cognitive signatures—is it truly, actively conscious beyond those words? We need to know *everything* it can tell us!" Even as she dove towards her instruments, her face alight with fierce concentration, he barked orders to his security detail, "Perimeter! Secure the shrine entrance! The Shivara cannot interrupt this—not now, not when we're on the threshold of such a monumental discovery!"

Lila's fingers danced across her interfaces, her eyes wide with a scientist's pure rapture as terabytes of unprecedented data flooded her systems. A breathless, triumphant laugh escaped her. "Commander, this is... this is beyond anything cataloged! It's not just a Keystone; it's an *event horizon* of new universal principles! The energy architecture, the resonance patterns, the sheer *coherence* of its output... it's... it's *more*! So much magnificently more!"

"More how, Lila?" Thorne pressed, his gaze flicking with barely contained excitement between Lila's ecstatic focus and the shadowy, now heavily guarded entrance to the shrine. "Give me something concrete!

The Shivara won't wait for us to publish our findings. Our window here is closing with every pulse of that thing—their fleet's detection of our presence is inevitable, and a prolonged engagement in this sacred, volatile space is unthinkable!"

"Understood, Commander!" Lila affirmed, her attention momentarily, brilliantly, shifting. "Eira! The Voice... Do you perceive anything further? Any continuation, any new resonance?"

Eira, still glowing with the residual energy of the profound contact, focused intently, her expression one of deep, wondrous concentration. "Just the humming now... but it's different. Deeper, more intricate. It feels... vast. Almost like it's... resting? Processing, perhaps, after that incredible declaration?"

Lila nodded, a thousand exhilarating theories already sparking and connecting in her mind. "Resting... after such an output! Fascinating! The energy expenditure alone must have been colossal!"

With a renewed burst of almost supernatural speed, her movements precise and incredibly swift, Lila moved between her array of scanners and recorders, a blur of focused motion. Eira and Erebus watched, captivated by her intensity, the air around her practically crackling with discovery. Minutes stretched, taut with the thrill of capturing the unknown. Then, abruptly, she stopped, a look of triumphant completion lighting her face.

"Commander! I have it!" she exclaimed, her voice ringing with elation. "I've captured a data stream of incredible density and complexity! We can't fully decode it here, the variables, the *novelty* of it all, are too immense. We need the stronghold's primary analytic core to even begin to understand the sheer scope of what we've just witnessed, what this Keystone *is*!"

"Affirmative, Lila! That's our cue!" Thorne's voice boomed with satisfaction and an urgent, thrilling anticipation. "All teams, extract! Rendezvous at the shrine entrance, now! We're taking this treasure trove of cosmic secrets home!"

The assembly was swift, a disciplined whirlwind of exhilarated activity, each member of the team aware they had been part of something historic. Moments later, they shimmered from the ancient shrine, reappearing on the transport pad of their orbiting vessel, the very deck plates seeming to hum with the residual energy of their discovery. The interstellar drive flared once more, and with that same breathtaking, near-instantaneous transition, the familiar, fortified architecture of the Bramah stronghold materialized around them.

The precious equipment was carefully, almost reverently, offloaded, the potential secrets it held almost crackling in the air like contained lightning. Eira and Erebus, still resonating with the shrine's potent energy and the Keystone's incredible words, were quickly and carefully escorted back to their specialized holding areas, their every vital sign, every subtle energy fluctuation, now a subject of even more intense, excited scrutiny. The universe had just spoken, and the Bramah had the recording.

Guardians of the Keystones: Echoes

Chapter Eleven

Thorne didn't pause, didn't even break stride from the transport bay, his boots echoing with swift, resonant purpose through the stronghold's hallowed corridors. The news he carried was too monumental, too universe-altering to delay by a single breath. He strode directly into Aethon's command sanctum, the very air around him seeming to crackle with the energy of what he'd witnessed.

"Commander!" Thorne's voice was charged, vibrant with the sheer, electrifying incredibility of their findings. "We have... an unprecedented report! The Prime Keystone at Elyria—it *spoke* to us again! It is undeniably, unequivocally a living entity! Something far beyond the nature of any other Keystone we have ever known, a power, a consciousness we've never conceived of before—until now!"

Aethon rose from his command chair, his formidable presence usually an unreadable mask of Bramah resolve, now visibly charged with profound astonishment and a dawning, intense excitement. "Living? *Spoke*?" He leaned forward, his eyes blazing with a light that mirrored the cosmic revelation Thorne described. "This changes *everything*, Thorne! The implications are staggering, potentially reshaping our entire understanding of the cosmos! Lila—was she successful? Did she capture the essence of this... this awakening?"

"Completely, Commander!" Thorne affirmed, a grin of pure, unadulterated exhilaration threatening to break his stern military composure. "An avalanche of data! More than we dared hope! Preliminarily, Lila theorizes that any significant manifestation, like direct communication, necessitates a... a recuperative phase for the Keystone. A resting cycle. As if it expends vast, almost unimaginable reserves of energy to interact and must then gather more." He leaned in, his voice dropping conspiratorially, alight with discovery. "And more intriguingly, Commander, the baseline energy readings suggest its overall power signature is... *incrementally increasing*. It's growing, sir. Becoming stronger!"

"Growing..." Aethon paced the sanctum, a new, almost boyish fire in his movements, the weight of ages momentarily lifted by the thrill of this paradigm shift. "Then we are on the absolute cusp of understanding a power beyond our most audacious reckoning! Thorne, your priority is now absolute: oversee Lila's analysis of this... this treasure. Every resource she requires is hers, without question. I want immediate updates on anything concrete, any discernible pattern, any insight into its nature, its intent, its very being!" He turned, his gaze locking with Thorne's, full of fervent purpose. "We must understand this phenomenon, Thorne! We must learn its rhythms, its potential! And yes," a new note of thrilling command entered his voice, "we must ensure its future awakenings are ones we can anticipate, perhaps even... guide. Future activations cannot be left to unmanaged chance. This is a new frontier, a new destiny for the Bramah!"

"It will be done, Commander!" Thorne declared, his spirit soaring, already turning, eager to rejoin the heart of the discovery where Lila was undoubtedly already unraveling miracles. He found her lab electric, a whirlwind of focused energy as the initial, colossal data streams began their journey into the stronghold's primary analytic systems. The very air thrummed with potential.

"Lila," Thorne's voice resonated with the Commander's potent urgency and his own fervent anticipation, "Aethon needs answers, and he needs them yesterday! The moment you have anything—anything at all that begins to unravel this magnificent mystery—you notify me. We are on the verge of something truly transformative!"

Within the deepest heart of the Shivara stronghold, where the architecture itself seemed carved from solidified Void, lay Kael's personal sanctuary. No light penetrated here save for the cold, internal luminescence of strange glyphs that pulsed rhythmically on obsidian walls, their glow reflecting in eyes that had witnessed the birth and death of galaxies. Kael, leader of the Shivara, sat enthroned, a figure of immense, coiled power, his form almost one with the oppressive shadows, his consciousness adrift in the silent, knowing expanse of the greater Void.

A chime, like the shattering of distant, frozen stars, resonated through the sanctuary, a dissonance in the perfect gloom. Cassius's image formed upon a barely visible interface, a stark, impassive emissary against the sanctuary's profound blackness.

"Lord Kael," the adjutant's synthesized voice was a sterile intrusion. "A signal, as anticipated from the lesser channels. It is the mortal, Lord Valerius."

A faint, almost imperceptible tightening around Kael's shadowed lips was his only reaction. Valerius. That persistent, posturing gnat, buzzing again at the edges of true power. "And what triviality does the 'Lord' of the Veil pester us with this cycle?" Kael's voice was the sound of ancient icebergs calving into a lightless sea, each word imbued with aeons of chilling disdain.

"He claims to have brokered access to intelligence, Lord Kael. Information regarding a Keystone of significant potency." Cassius paused, a micro-fraction of a second that somehow conveyed the distastefulness of the messenger. "He wishes to present another mortal, one who purportedly holds this information, seeking to barter it for an audience."

Kael's shadowed head tilted, a slow, deliberate movement. "Valerius, ever the ambitious scavenger, ferrying trinkets he barely understands in the hope of scraps from a greater table. And now he brings another, equally blind, to offer up a prize he cannot truly grasp." A dark amusement, colder than the Void itself, touched Kael's tone. "A Keystone... Interesting that such a fragment of primal order should fall into the trembling hands of such... *insects*." He considered for a moment, the silence in the sanctuary growing deeper, heavier. "No matter. The knowledge itself may have utility, regardless of the messenger's squalor. Indulge Valerius's preening. Arrange the presentation. This new mortal... let us see what it has to offer before its fleeting relevance is exhausted."

"It will be done, Lord Kael." Cassius's image flickered once, then vanished, plunging the sanctuary back into its profound, undisturbed darkness. Kael remained, a silent colossus of shadow, Valerius already dismissed from his thoughts, the mortal informant merely a new, temporary variable in the Shivara's vast and patient equations of power. Their offerings would be taken, their hopes consumed, and the great, silent Void would endure.

The stronghold's primary analytic core roared to life, a contained sun devouring the terabytes of unprecedented data from Elyria. Above Lila's lab, on the observation deck, Thorne paced like a caged thunderbolt, the energy from the Prime Keystone's revelation still coursing through him. Below, Lila was a maestro conducting an orchestra of light and information, her commands flying across holographic interfaces, her eyes alight with the dazzling, intricate dance of algorithms deciphering cosmic enigmas.

"Commander!" Lila's voice crackled over the comms, pure, unadulterated exhilaration making it sharp and bright, cutting through the thrum of the machinery. "The primary parse is complete! The models are… they're breathtaking! The dynamic interplay, the sheer sophistication of its energy matrices linked to what can only be described as conscious output—Thorne, there's *nothing* like this in any known record, in any theory! We've stepped into entirely new territory of existence!"

Thorne was at her side in an instant, leaning over the console, his own gaze fixed on the swirling, incandescent data streams that painted galaxies of information across the main display. "Actionable, Lila! Aethon will demand more than awe—he'll want understanding, leverage! How quickly can we translate this spectacle into something we can *use*, something that gives us an edge, a true insight into its will?"

"The volume is astronomical, Commander, but our systems are *singing* with this data! They're resonating with it!" Lila declared, her fingers a blur across the controls, new diagnostic windows flaring into existence. "Key resonance signatures, the very fingerprints of its thought process, are isolating as we speak! The first truly coherent insights—our first genuine glimpse into the *mind* of the Prime Keystone—will be ours inside the hour! Prepare yourself, Commander, the universe is about to get a whole lot bigger!"

The minutes stretched, each one thrumming with the vibrant hum of the analytic core and the almost unbearable, electric weight of anticipation. Every technician in the extended lab held their breath, eyes glued to their dedicated consoles, acutely aware they were witnessing the birth of a new understanding, a moment that would redefine Bramah knowledge forever. Lila, a whirlwind of focused intensity, pushed the systems to their limits, her mind racing in tandem with the processors, a pioneer on the very precipice of the known universe.

Suddenly—a sharp, almost explosive indrawn breath from Lila. Her eyes, already wide with fervent concentration, dilated further as the primary console before her erupted with a cascade of fully resolved, breathtakingly intricate reports. The patterns locked, the algorithms converged, the truth unveiled itself in a torrent of light and meaning!

"Thorne!" Her voice was a hushed torrent of disbelief and raw, unadulterated triumph, a herald of the incredible. "The Prime Keystone's consciousness... it's not just *aware* in a passive sense! It's a colossal, interconnected *symphony* of cognitive functions! We're looking at what might be a unified intelligence, Commander, networked across dimensions we can barely theorize about! Think of the sheer scale!" She gestured wildly at the screen, which now displayed a stunning, multi-layered, almost organic map of interconnected energy nodes and pathways, pulsing with an inner light. "Each output spike, every activation we've ever recorded from *any* Keystone, but especially *this* Prime one—it appears to be a meticulously coordinated effort! An overarching, almost incomprehensible will, Thorne, capable of exerting its influence, its very *being*, across the fabric of multiple realities simultaneously! We are witnessing the operational mind of a cosmic architect!"

Within Elyon's radiant sanctum, a subtle disturbance in the ambient cosmic energies signaled Kronos's return. He materialized before the Fount of Creation, his presence carrying the weight of his journey through the currents of time.

"What have you learned from your passage through time, Kronos?" Elyon inquired, His voice calm and deeply resonant. **"What truths has your search revealed?"**

Kronos inclined his head, his form imbued with the ancient light of distant stars. **"Great Architect,"** his words carried the gravity of his findings, **"those mortals who bear the singular Shard-Heart... within them reside the core life-essences of the First Pair you shaped at the beginning of this creation. It appears the Shard-Heart was drawn to them not by chance, but by the unique signature of Your original design for humanity."**

Elyon considered this, His divine aura subtly shifting with contemplation. **"And why would the Prime Keystone, now stirring with its own awareness, seek out these echoes of Our first mortal creations?"**

"The full design is not yet clear, Divine Elyon," Kronos stated, his sight encompassing vast sweeps of probability and consequence. **"But the indications are that the Keystone, now sentient, may see in these original life-essences a unique means to interact with the physical realm—perhaps even to form a vessel for its consciousness. As the template for humanity, they might be the only forms it deems suitable or capable for its purpose."**

A deeper resonance emanated from Elyon, His customary serenity touched by the gravity of the unfolding situation. **"We must understand its ultimate goal, Kronos. The Bramah require our guidance, and the stability of Order is threatened by this uncertainty. Time is not on our side in this matter."**

"I understand, Father of All," Kronos affirmed, his form already beginning to lose definition as he prepared to re-engage with the vast currents of time. **"I will continue to seek the answers within the flows of past and future. Time will yield what we need to know."**

With that, his presence faded from Elyon's chambers, leaving the God of Creation to His contemplations in the enduring, serene light of His domain.

At Elyon's call, a presence swifter than starlight yet softer than shadow materialized within His radiant chambers. Nyx, a trusted emissary whose form shimmered with an inner luminescence, bowed low before the Fount of Creation.

"Nyx, swift messenger," Elyon's voice, calm yet imbued with an undeniable gravity, filled the sanctum. **"You must bear critical tidings to Aethon of the Bramah. Inform him thus: the Shard-Heart, in its divided aspects, was drawn to the mortal vessels, Eira and Erebus, not by mere chance. Those two embody the very**

essence, the core life-spark, of the First Pair I shaped in the dawn of ages – the genesis of mortal kind throughout the cosmos."

Nyx absorbed the profound words, her luminous form still held in deep reverence. **"My Lord Elyon, this is a revelation of immense weight. Such a connection is... profound. But if I may seek clarity, what purpose would the Prime Keystone then have in seeking out these... original essences through them?"**

"That ultimate design remains veiled, even from Us for now, dear Nyx," Elyon replied, a flicker of cosmic concern, like a distant nebula dimming, touching His gaze. **"Kronos himself delves into the currents of time seeking that answer. Yet, this Aethon *must* comprehend with all urgency: caution is paramount in their dealings with these mortals. Should the twin aspects of the Shard-Heart within them unite without guidance, without true understanding of the forces at play... the potential for unbridled chaos, cascading across the very fabric of the multiverse, is a dire possibility we cannot ignore."**

"I understand the gravity, Divine One," Nyx affirmed, her voice earnest and clear. **"I will convey this sacred knowledge and your solemn warning to Commander Aethon without delay. He will be made aware of the stakes."**

"Go swiftly then, child of light," Elyon urged, His luminous presence imbuing her with a sense of profound, pressing purpose. **"The balance is delicate, and awareness is their sharpest shield."**

Nyx bowed once more, a gesture of absolute fealty, then turned. With a speed that defied mortal perception, her light resolved into a streak of focused energy, dissolving from the chamber, already on her swift journey through the pathways between realms to the Bramah stronghold.

The oppressive normalcy of the City Archives building behind her offered no comfort as Nalini plunged into the waiting maw of the pre-arranged alleyway. Here, nestled between indifferent, grimy municipal walls, the late morning sun was a forgotten rumor, choked out by a chilling gloom that clung to the damp brickwork and reeked of stale refuse and urban despair. Each hesitant footstep echoed unnaturally, magnified by the narrow passage.

Deeper within, where shadows congealed into an almost solid blackness near overflowing dumpsters, a figure detached itself from the wall. Raven Locke. Her stillness had been absolute, part of the alley's decay, making Nalini jump with a stifled gasp as if a predatory gargoyle had stirred to life. Her eyes, even in the dim, fetid light, held a sharp, expectant gleam.

"The air here is... unwholesome. As is my patience," Raven's voice was a silken rasp, seeming to coil out from the deepest shadows like a venomous serpent. "Your findings, informant. They had best justify this squalid rendezvous. Quickly."

Nalini pressed herself against the cold, gritty brick, the data chip a slippery, fragile thing in her sweating palm. The alley felt like a closing fist, the stench of decay making her want to retch. "The... Umbra Collective..." she began, each word a fearful exhalation that barely disturbed the stagnant, heavy air. Her voice was a thin thread, easily lost. "They are... ancient, my lady. Centuries old, perhaps far longer. Cloaked in an impenetrable secrecy." She could feel Raven's unblinking stare, a physical weight in the claustrophobic space. "Operatives... they are like unseen spiders, their webs spun throughout the sector. Their obsession is... forbidden knowledge. Arcane truths, sciences lost to sensible minds, horrors best left interred. They gather it, hoard it... and through this dark accumulation, their influence, their insidious power, apparently festers and expands." Nalini's voice faltered, the oppressive atmosphere and Raven's nearness making it hard to breathe. "That is... all I could confidently unearth. So much is veiled, my lady. Their roots run into the deepest, blackest soil; their secrets are entombed beneath layers of silence and profound terror."

Raven took a silent step closer, the scant distance between them shrinking to nothing, her presence eclipsing the alley's faint, grimy light filtering from its distant mouth. Her breath, cool and odorless, ghosted across Nalini's cheek. "Here, in this filth," Raven's whisper was colder than the damp stones beneath their feet, "lies are so easily... disposed of. Along with those who peddle them. If you have wasted my time with fictions woven from your own fear, informant, your end will be as anonymous and unmourned as the refuse that chokes this gutter."

"No, I... I swear it is what I believe to be the truth!" Nalini stammered, terror making her words brittle, desperate to appease the shadow before her. "The patterns... the redactions... the whispers... they all point to this terrifying reality!"

A small, heavy packet of untraceable credits skittered across the greasy cobblestones, landing with a dull thud near a pile of sodden, forgotten refuse. A final, contemptuous offering. Then, as swiftly and silently as she had materialized from them, Raven Locke stepped back, and the consuming darkness at the alley's deeper end simply... swallowed her. She was gone, leaving Nalini utterly alone, heart hammering against her ribs as if trying to escape. The sudden silence was broken only by a distant, mocking city siren. The stench of decay and her own cold fear were suddenly overwhelming, and the weight of the knowledge she now possessed settled upon her like a burial shroud.

Raven Locke manifested from the deepest shadows clinging to the utilitarian structures of the Aurora Initiative's docking bay, a sliver of true night intruding upon its sterile, overlit functionality. Her approach to the guarded entrance was that of a phantom, each step silent, her presence an immediate, chilling disruption to the mundane routine.

"I require an audience with Adrian Volkov," her voice was a low obsidian caress, devoid of inflection yet carrying an undeniable, cold authority. "Inform him I am here. Now."

One guard, visibly unnerved by her sudden appearance and the unnerving aura she projected, fumbled with the comm panel. His hushed, urgent words to Dr. Volkov were met with a swift, affirmative reply. The heavy blast door hissed open with a reluctant groan, and the guard, careful to avoid her gaze, gestured her into a long, echoing corridor bathed in harsh, unforgiving light. Raven moved through it like a stain, out of place and menacing.

Volkov's office was a stark contrast, a pocket of controlled quiet. He shut the door behind her himself, the click of the lock sounding unnaturally loud. An almost imperceptible tremor of anticipation, or perhaps something else, touched his otherwise composed features. "Your... principal," Volkov began, his voice a carefully modulated baritone, "has he found my proposal... amenable?"

"Lord Valerius awaits your presence," Raven stated, her eyes like chips of frozen void. "I am to escort you. Immediately."

A flicker of triumph, sharp and dangerous, crossed Volkov's face. "Excellent."

"Are you... prepared?" Raven's question was less a concern and more a final, chilling assessment.

"Entirely."

With a barely perceptible nod, Raven extended a hand, not to touch him, but towards the oppressive shadow that inexplicably pooled and deepened behind her, even in the well-lit office. "Then come." She stepped into it, and the shadow seemed to rise, to *embrace* her. With her hand now briefly on Volkov's shoulder, the world dissolved for him into a sickening, freezing plunge through non-space, a wrenching passage through utter blackness that tore at his senses.

Within heartbeats that felt like frozen eternities, they emerged, stumbling slightly, into the profound, sepulchral chill deep beneath the earth – the lightless heart of the Order of the Veil's stronghold. The air was thick, tasting of ancient stone, forgotten rituals, and a pervasive, underlying malice. Raven, already moving, gestured with a subtle inclination of her head for him to follow. Her silent passage down the Stygian hallways was that of a native creature, while Volkov felt each step pull him deeper into a waiting tomb.

Lord Valerius was a denser knot of darkness upon his throne of shadows in the central sanctum, his form barely distinguishable yet radiating an almost palpable aura of ancient, cruel power. Raven approached him first, a wraith deferring to a greater abyss. Her whispered words, detailing her findings on the Umbra Collective, were too low for Volkov to discern, but he saw the faintest, most terrifying curve of what might have been a smile touch Valerius's unseen lips – a predator's brief, satisfied rictus. Then, that chilling attention focused, laser-like, upon him.

"So," Valerius's voice slithered from the darkness, like the rasp of stone on stone, ancient and utterly devoid of warmth. "You are the mortal who presumes to seek an audience with our... patrons. What precious secrets do you imagine yourself to possess, that would render you worthy of such a blasphemous honor?"

Volkov, though visibly paling in the oppressive presence, held his ground, a desperate gambler playing his final, highest stake. "I wish to share the extensive knowledge my Umbra Collective holds. Regarding the Keystone the Bramah are currently... fumbling with."

A dry, rustling sound, like dead leaves skittering across a crypt floor – Valerius's version of a chuckle. "We are already... aware... of this particular bauble, mortal."

"Perhaps some fragments," Volkov countered, a dangerous edge to his own voice now. "But we possess a far deeper, more intimate understanding than even the great Bramah. Unless, of course, you would prefer we enlighten *them* instead?"

The air in the sanctum seemed to drop several degrees further. "You tread on treacherous ground, little spark of ambition," Valerius's voice was a silken threat. "Ensure this 'knowledge' does not merely waste Our irreplaceable time. The cost for such an error... would be exquisite, and eternal."

"I assure you, Lord Valerius," Volkov managed, his voice tight but firm, "you will not be... disappointed." The unspoken words hung heavy: *and I pray I survive this assurance.*

Guardians of the Keystones: Echoes

Chapter Twelve

Aethon stood before the grand star-map in his private sanctum, the silent, swirling galaxies reflecting the somber weight of his thoughts. Suddenly, the chamber filled with a soft, silver luminescence, a celestial light that did not cast shadows but dispelled them. From this gentle radiance, the divine form of Nyx manifested, her presence a balm of serene power and ancient starlight.

"**Aethon, First of the Bramah,**" Nyx's voice was like the chime of distant, sacred bells, a sound that resonated not in the ear, but in the soul. "**I am come to you, bearing urgent word and sacred insight from the Divine Elyon.**"

Aethon turned, his face a mask of profound awe, and immediately knelt, bowing his head before the divine messenger. "Radiant Nyx. My being is humbled by your presence. I am here to receive your wisdom."

"**Rise, steadfast Aethon,**" she urged, her voice imbued with a gentle yet undeniable authority. "**This truth requires your full attention, for it alters all you have presumed.**"

As he stood, his gaze reverently fixed upon her, Nyx continued, her voice resonating with divine clarity. "**The Shard-Heart, in its divided aspects, did not alight upon the mortals Eira and Erebus by chance. They were sought, drawn by an ancient, sacred reso-**

nance. For within them, Aethon, flows the pure, original essence of the First Pair—the very wellspring of life from which the Divine Elyon first designed mortal kind. They are living echoes of Creation's dawn."

She paused, letting the immense weight of this revelation settle upon him. "**It is Our belief that the awakening Prime Keystone, in its vast sentience, perceives in them a unique potential: a conduit through which to shape a vessel for its own consciousness, that it might break the bonds of its current form and find a new freedom within the realms.**"

Aethon's eyes widened, his tactical mind giving way to profound, astonished comprehension. "Then its sentience is absolute. The Keystone truly *lives*."

"**It does,**" Nyx confirmed, her expression turning solemn, reflecting the gravity of her message. "**Even now, the great Kronos delves into the currents of time for deeper clarity. But your charge from Elyon is this: the mortals must be kept as they are. Do not allow them to be separated, for the tension between their essences holds a delicate, necessary balance. Yet, do not, under any circumstance, permit them direct physical contact. The uncontrolled reunion of those original essences, the raw merging of the Shard-Heart's aspects... it could unleash a dissonance so great it would threaten to unravel the very fabric of the multiverse.**"

Her luminous gaze intensified. "**Furthermore, you must shield them—and the Prime Keystone at Elyria—with all the might of the Bramah. Should they fall to the servants of the Great Darkness or their Shivara thralls, all that We have wrought could be unmade in an age of despair.**"

"Your will, and the will of the Divine Elyon, shall be my command, Radiant One," Aethon declared, his voice ringing with renewed, sacred purpose, his doubts washed away by the clarity of divine instruction. "I will see it done."

Nyx nodded, a soft, approving light seeming to emanate from her. **"Be vigilant, noble Aethon. The weight of countless worlds rests once more upon the shoulders of the Bramah. We place Our divine trust in you."**

Aethon bowed his head once more in deepest reverence, and when he looked up, Nyx was gone. The silver light receded like a fading star, leaving only the faint, sweet scent of distant nebulae and the profound gravity of his new, holy charge.

The alien contours of the Bramah communication device seemed to absorb the sterile light in Dr. Elijah Thompson's lab, a dark, unsettling intrusion of impossible science. He leaned closer, his own reflection a ghostly, worried mask on its polished, dark surface.

"Maya," he hissed, his voice barely a whisper, gesturing her over with a short, jerky movement. "Look at these readings. Now."

Maya Singh hurried to his side, her professional curiosity quickly souring into a chilling dread as she scanned the cascading, unfamiliar data on the device's screen. She looked up from the pad, her eyes wide, the color draining from her face.

"The energy signatures... Elijah, they're off any conceivable scale. This isn't just powerful; it's... existential. Our most advanced sensors wouldn't even register this properly, they'd just burn out."

"Exactly," Elijah muttered, running a hand through his already disheveled hair, his gaze darting towards the corridor as if expecting shadows to lengthen there. "And according to Lila's own annotated files, even the *Bramah*—the immortal, god-serving Bramah—are effectively staring into the sun, trying not to be blinded by its power." He pointed a trembling finger at a specific data point, a jagged spike of pure insanity. "That flux, right there? That's what caused the temporal anomaly in our own system logs last week. A flicker from that thing, and our timeline... *hiccuped*. Another one, Maya, a bigger one... it could just erase us." His voice dropped further, thick with paranoia. "And do they have it under control? Do they even truly know what it is they're dealing with?"

"They *believe* they have a handle on it," Maya whispered back, her own eyes scanning the supposedly empty lab with newfound suspicion. "For now. But long-term? Lila's own projections are... chaotic. Unpredictable."

"That's what I can't shake," Elijah said, his gaze becoming hard, focused. "We need to keep this data locked down. All of it. Compartmentalized. Because I don't trust Adrian Volkov." The name hung in the air between them like a toxin. "There's something... predatory about him. About the way his personal guard moves, the way they watch everyone. They don't act like Aurora Initiative security, Maya. They act like wardens."

Maya nodded, her expression grim, her mind racing. "I agree. We have to warn the others on our team—the ones who were there, who saw what we saw. Keep what we experienced off-world, our interactions with the Bramah, completely confidential. Until we know who we can actually trust inside these walls." She looked around again, the clean, minimalist lines of the lab suddenly feeling like the bars of a cage. "But how do we do that without raising alarms? Volkov's people have eyes everywhere."

"We act normal," Elijah insisted, his voice low and firm, a desperate plan forming. "We go about our duties. No sudden changes in routine. But we talk, quietly. We find out who else feels it—this undercurrent of... *wrongness*." He met her gaze, a silent, fearful pact passing between them.

They moved with a newfound, deliberate caution for the rest of the day, their conversations quiet murmurs in shielded corridors, a shared, meaningful look across a crowded cafeteria. One by one, they passed on the warning to their trusted colleagues, their words hushed whispers of caution against an unseen threat within their own organization.

Later, alone in his lab, Elijah began building new, deeper layers of encryption around the Bramah data, walling off the terrible, magnificent truth from prying eyes he could feel but not see. He knew, with a certainty that chilled him to the bone, that a serpent was coiled within the heart of the Aurora Initiative. He just didn't know how many heads it had, or when it would finally choose to strike.

The sterile quiet of the lab was a lie, a thin veneer over the frantic hammering of Elijah Thompson's own heart. He could feel the weight of unseen eyes, a prickling certainty at the back of his neck that had festered for days into a low-grade, simmering paranoia. Every line of encryption he feverishly built felt like a desperate sandbag against a rising, invisible tide. Were Volkov's people watching? Was the feed from his own terminal being mirrored on some hidden screen? The thought made his fingers slick with a cold sweat.

A low thrum. The consistent hum of the server banks suddenly dropped in pitch, a subtle, gut-wrenching wrongness that vibrated through the floor. Elijah froze, his hands hovering over the holographic interface. His eyes darted to the corner of the room, where the shadows thrown by a server rack seemed unnaturally deep, no longer just an absence of light, but a presence.

The corner didn't just darken; it seemed to *deepen*, to gain an impossible, predatory depth. From that spreading void, a figure resolved itself, stepping not *out* of the shadow but seemingly woven from its very fabric. A woman, whose profound stillness was a vortex in the room, sucking all noise and certainty into it. Elijah's breath hitched, a choked knot of pure, adrenaline-fueled terror in his throat.

"Dr. Thompson." Her voice was impossibly low and calm, yet it cut through the hum of the lab, a sound as sharp and cold as a scalpel. "Your alarm is a logical, but unnecessary, reaction. My name is Dasyra. I am of the Bramah."

She took a single, perfectly silent step forward, her presence dominating the room. "Commander Aethon is aware of your... predicament. We have observed the digital phantoms you chase through your own security protocols. The knowledge you protect is of cosmic importance. Its sanctity must be maintained."

"The Bramah..." Elijah stammered, his scientific mind struggling to reconcile the impossible figure before him with the laws of physics she had just flagrantly violated. "How...?" He took a deep, shuddering breath, the words tumbling out in a hushed, desperate torrent. "We're... concerned about a man. Adrian Volkov. He shouldn't be here. He appeared after the last activation of the Prime Keystone—he's an anomaly, a ghost in our timeline, and he's consolidating power with terrifying speed."

A flicker of confirmation, as cold and distant as starlight, passed through Dasyra's unreadable eyes. She produced a small, crystalline device that seemed to pull the lab's artificial light into itself, casting a chilling, mobile shadow around her hand. "Then our objectives are aligned."

She placed the device on Elijah's terminal. There was no interface, no connection. Instantly, the lights in the lab dimmed for a split second, and a wave of palpable cold, like static electricity, washed over Elijah. The terminal screen flared with a blinding web of intricate, glowing glyphs before returning to normal.

"The data is now veiled," Dasyra stated, her voice a flat, factual counterpoint to the terrifying display of power. "It is shielded from any technology forged in this epoch. Furthermore, any attempt to breach the veil will register not as a simple log, but as a direct, instantaneous distress call to us."

"But *why*?" Elijah whispered, staring at the alien artifact, a piece of impossible, divine science now sitting inertly on his desk. "What is his motive? Something is fundamentally wrong here, I can feel it."

"That is the question I am here to answer," Dasyra replied, her form already seeming to blur at the edges as she retreated toward the corner she had emerged from. Her voice was a chilling promise that lingered in the air. "Ignorance is a wound left to fester. I can walk the unseen paths between whispers. I will learn his intent."

And as Elijah watched, paralyzed, she turned and stepped directly into a shadow that should have been no deeper than a hand's breadth, and simply... vanished. The oppressive silence she left behind was a new kind of terror, now laced with a horrifying, yet undeniable, sliver of hope.

In the lowest, most lightless sanctum of the Order of the Veil, where the stones themselves seemed saturated with ancient dread, Volkov and Lord Valerius stood as silent effigies. Between them, the mystic Nightshade swayed, her face obscured by a deep cowl, her voice a sibilant hiss, whispering incantations that felt like hairline fractures spreading across the fabric of reality itself.

Before her, space did not open; it *tore*. A ragged, weeping wound of absolute blackness bled into the chamber, a portal that did not show stars but devoured light, exuding a silence so profound it was a physical pressure, a suffocating cold that promised only oblivion.

From the depths of that abyssal tear, a face coalesced—Niamh of the Shivara. Her image was pristine yet fundamentally unstable, laced with veins of shimmering, predatory static, her eyes ancient pits of cold starlight. Her voice was not a sound that crossed the chamber but a telepathic imposition, a spike of ice driven directly into their minds.

"Why do you scratch at the door of the Void, little acolyte of shadows? You reek of desperation, Valerius."

Lord Valerius bowed his head, a gesture of profound but hollow deference, the oppressive presence of the Shivara seeming to physically weigh him down. "Great Niamh," his voice was a strained whisper, "we sought this audience only to present a... resource. A mortal who professes to hold knowledge regarding a Keystone—the one that currently vexes the servants of Order."

Niamh's projected face remained a mask of cosmic indifference, her utter contempt a palpable force. *"We are aware of the anchor. And you bring us... chattering dust. We have no use for the deluded pronouncements of ephemeral beings. Erase this one from existence and cease your mewling at our threshold. Do not disturb us again with such trivialities."*

Before Valerius could even formulate a response to the crushing dismissal, Volkov stepped forward into the full, chilling focus of the Shivara's gaze. His voice, shockingly clear and steady in the dreadful silence, cut through the air. "Forgive this intrusion, Great Niamh. I am Adrian Volkov. I represent the Umbra Collective, not merely this Order." He did not bow. "The information is not a fragment. We know the Aurora Initiative collaborates with the Bramah. We know they hold a mortal woman whose very life-essence is intrinsically, physically tied to this Keystone. We can deliver this woman to you. A living key, Great Niamh. A means to not just observe the lock, but to *control* it."

A long, agonizing silence stretched, so heavy it felt as if the very stones of the sanctum might crack. Niamh's eyes narrowed, the starlight within them seeming to collapse into black holes of pure, calculating thought.

"Insolence... to address Us directly." A flicker of something that might have been cruel, predatory interest crossed her face. *"And yet... a living key. A concept of some... merit. Your tiny flicker of existence is spared, Adrian Volkov. For now."* Her gaze shifted back to Valerius, sharp and utterly dismissive. *"But be warned: the Shivara do not suffer fools, and our disappointment is... absolute. He will deliver this intelligence to you, Valerius. Do not trouble us again until you hold something of tangible worth in your trembling hands. The door you have knocked upon is not one you truly wish to see opened fully."*

With that final, chilling edict, Niamh's image dissolved. The weeping wound in reality sealed itself with a soundless, violent implosion, leaving behind an even deeper cold and the stench of ozone and dread. Lord Valerius turned on Volkov, the shadows around him seeming to writhe and clench, his voice a low, venomous snarl.

"You will deliver *everything*. Now. Pray to whatever pathetic gods you cherish that what you have offered is enough to sate them. Because the suffering I will inflict upon you should they be displeased will make you beg for the simple, clean oblivion they would have granted you moments ago."

Raven Locke materialized from the gloom behind Volkov, her presence a silent, final command. It was time for him to leave the tomb—for now.

Niamh materialized within the suffocating stillness of Kael's sanctuary, her form a stark, disciplined silhouette against the Void-touched glyphs that pulsed with a cold, internal light. She knelt, her head bowed, a subordinate before an ancient power.

"Lord Kael," she announced, her voice a low, dispassionate chime that was absorbed by the profound silence. "I bring a report, as commanded."

Kael's presence, a gravity well of pure thought that dominated the chamber, acknowledged her without physical movement. His voice was not a sound, but a direct, chilling imposition of will upon her mind. *"Speak."*

"The tendril from the Order of the Veil made contact," Niamh began, her report concise and devoid of emotion. "Valerius acted as the conduit."

"The Valerius pest," Kael's thought reverberated, a statement of fact, not of anger. *"What consequence could its frantic scrabbling possibly hold for the Shivara?"*

"He served only to present another mortal," Niamh clarified, her gaze fixed on the obsidian floor. "One Adrian Volkov, who claims to represent an entity known as the Umbra Collective. This mortal asserts possession of extensive data regarding the Prime Keystone—intelligence, he purports, that rivals or exceeds that of the Bramah. He offers this knowledge, and himself as a permanent liaison, in exchange for our... consideration."

A silence stretched, heavy and absolute, as Kael processed this. *"And you brushed against its mind? You verified the substance of this claim?"*

"I did, my Lord," Niamh confirmed. "The mortal's mind is... disciplined. Shielded in a way that suggests formal training. I could not breach his core consciousness from the distance required by the Void-link. However, I perceived the surface layers: conviction, ambition, and the undeniable belief that the data he holds is of profound value. The shields themselves are a testament that something of worth is being protected. With physical proximity," she added, a hint of her own formidable power touching her tone, "I am certain his mental fortitude would crumble."

"So be it," Kael's will settled upon her, as cold and final as the heat death of a universe. *"Proceed with the transaction. Let the Valerius pest broker this exchange. But be clear, Niamh. If this proves to be a deception, if their offering is worthless... extinguish them. Both the mortal and his handler. Do not permit their failure to waste another moment of our time."*

"It shall be as you command, Lord Kael."

Niamh bowed deeply once more, a gesture of absolute, unquestioning obedience. Her form then dissolved back into the perfect, oppressive darkness of the sanctuary, leaving Kael to the silent contemplation of cosmic machinations and the trivial, predictable dance of ambitious, short-lived mortals.

Guardians of the Keystones:
Echoes

Chapter Thirteen

In a realm where the concept of light was a forgotten, blasphemous heresy, where the Void itself was tortured into a monument of eternal agony, Zarathos slouched upon a throne of coalesced dread and crystallized despair. The "air," if it could be called such, carried the faint, unending psychic echo of dying stars and the quiet weeping of broken hope.

With a mere flicker of his ancient, hateful will, space before the throne warped and tore open. From that violent rupture, Tharros, the God of Domination and Control, was violently wrenched from his own dark contemplations to kneel, his form a groveling tapestry of living chains and suffocating shadow that scraped against the obsidian floor.

"My will is yours, Eternal Blight," Tharros's thought groveled, a wave of absolute, soul-crushed subjugation.

Zarathos's own thought was a wave of pure malevolence that made Tharros flinch, a voice that was the grinding of tombstones. *"The insects of Order... the Bramah... tell me of their frantic, meaningless scurrying. Report."*

"They swarm around a relic, Master," Tharros reported, his head bowed so low it touched the floor. *"A Keystone of significant power, located in the tamer, structured realms. It has pulsed twice with no-*

table energy, creating ruptures in the placid fabric of their reality. It is not yet known if their pathetic meddling caused these activations, or if they are merely drawn to the scent of power like flies to a corpse."

"A source of their stability... a linchpin of their tedious reality..." A slow, terrible amusement radiated from Zarathos, a feeling like the cold touch of a blade tracing a line across flesh. *"Such a thing should not be wasted on mere balance. It must be taught new songs. Songs of despair, of exquisite corruption. It could become a beautiful instrument to amplify Our hold, to turn their precious multiverse into a symphony of endless, weeping screams."*

His will sharpened into a command, a spike of pure, nihilistic intent.

"Unleash the Shivara," Zarathos decreed, the words dripping with utter contempt for all lesser beings. *"Direct those hungry dogs to this plaything. Have them learn its secrets, then rip it from the Bramah's clutching, sanctimonious hands. I want it. Its potential for generating misery must not be squandered. Let there be no price too great in its acquisition. Let worlds burn if they must."*

Tharros did not look up. He felt the command settle into his very being, a brand of absolute purpose.

"Yes, Master. Their hope will be unmade."

Back within the sterile, oppressive quiet of his administrative sanctum in the Umbra Collective, Adrian Volkov allowed himself a rare, thin smile. The gambit had been perilous, the sheer audacity of it breathtaking, but it had worked. He had the attention of the Shivara. Now, all that remained was to deliver the promised offering. He settled into his high-backed chair, his fingers moving with practiced, efficient grace as he keyed the access codes for the Keystone data into his terminal.

The screen blinked back at him: QUERY RETURNED 0 RE-SULTS.

Volkov frowned, the smile vanishing. A mis-categorization? An archival error? He broadened the search parameters, running a root-level diagnostic, his irritation simmering. Still nothing. The system returned only a flat, digital void. Starting to feel a prickle of genuine concern, he patched in his assistant, his voice clipped and impatient.

"Rania, I require the primary data packet on Project Keystone. My terminal isn't locating it. Find it."

He waited, tapping a restless, sharp rhythm on the polished obsidian of his desk. The seconds stretched into a full minute, each one heavier than the last. Her voice finally came back over the comm, hesitant, laced with a new nervousness that set his teeth on edge.

"Sir... I can't find it either. I've run multiple searches. There's... no record of the file designation you provided. It's not just moved; it's as if it never existed."

A cold knot began to form in Volkov's gut. This was impossible. He bypassed his internal comms, opening a secure, encrypted channel directly to his head of security back at the Aurora Initiative, the data's source.

"This is Volkov," he snapped, dispensing with all pleasantries. "Report on the Keystone files. Has their security status been altered without my authorization?"

The voice on the other end was tense. "No, sir. No changes logged. All security protocols are green."

"Then why can I not access them?" Volkov demanded, his voice dangerously low, a coiled threat.

There was a pause filled with the frantic sound of virtual keys clicking. The silence stretched, screaming.

"Well?" Volkov's patience shredded.

"The files are gone, sir."

"What do you *mean*, 'gone'?" Volkov roared, his composure finally cracking, his voice echoing in the silent office. "Deleted? Archived under a new designation? Spit it out, man!"

"No, sir, I... I can't explain it," the security head stammered, fear now naked in his voice. "There's no trace of a deletion. No log of a transfer or unauthorized access. The data isn't just missing from the server; the space it occupied, the directory paths, the archival backups... they're all gone. It's like a surgical excision from reality itself. There's no ghost in the machine, sir. There's just... nothing."

"Who accessed them last?" Volkov's question was a desperate, final grasp at logic.

"That's the thing, sir," the voice on the other end was a terrified whisper. "According to the system, no one has. The access logs for that directory are blank. They simply... ceased to exist."

Volkov slowly lowered the comm device, the connection severing with a soft click that sounded like a gunshot in the suffocating silence of his office. *Gone. No trace.* A promise made to the monstrous Lord Valerius, a vow sworn under the chilling, soul-crushing gaze of the Shivara, and the price he had offered was now... nothing. A phantom. The cold knot in his stomach tightened into an iron vise of pure, visceral terror. His life hung by the thread of that data, and someone—or something—had just silently, impossibly, cut the line.

Eira drifted toward the transparent partition that separated their spaces, a silent invitation. From the shadows of his own enclosure, Erebus looked up, and without a word, walked to meet her on the other side. They stood inches apart, separated by the shimmering containment field, yet closer than anyone else in the universe.

She reached out with a thought, a gentle touch to his mind, soft as a held breath. *"How are you, Erebus? Is your... inner storm calm today?"*

His mental voice answered, the usual guarded edges softened by a quiet sincerity. *"It is, for now. I was just thinking... I know the darkness that shaped me. But you remain a mystery of light. You know my story, Eira. Now, please... show me yours."*

A tender, sad smile touched Eira's lips, and she opened her heart to him. She didn't just tell him; she let him *see.*

She shared the warmth of her early life in the beautiful city-state of Aethelburg, a bastion of strength on the dark but beloved world of Khyber. She let him feel the warmth of her mother's embrace and see the proud, loving smile of her father, a commander in the noble Stone Guard. She shared with him her most cherished possession: the small, smooth crystal shard they had given her. And then, she let him hear its song—not the mournful hum it was now, but the pure, gentle lullaby it used to sing to her as a child, a melody of absolute peace and unconditional love.

Then, with a shared, silent breath, she let the warmth of the memory chill. She shared the terror of that final day, when dark beings from the Void tore through their defenses. She didn't just show him a battle; she let him feel the heart-wrenching moment she saw her father fall, a giant of strength and love, struck down defending their home. She shared the searing pain of losing her mother in the chaos, her small hand slipping away into a sea of terrified, orphaned children.

She then guided him through the disorienting blur of her arrival on Solara, and the slow, crushing descent into the lower levels of Acarcis. He felt her awe at the impossible scale of the city curdle into fear as she was swallowed by its perpetual, rain-slicked twilight, choked by the psychic noise and raw desperation of millions.

He felt her gentle, empathetic nature, amplified by her Shard, turn into a curse. He experienced the overwhelming assault of the city's collective anguish—the anger, the greed, the fear—a constant scream that she had no choice but to endure. He watched through her eyes as she learned to make herself invisible, a ghost in the crowd, a small, huddled figure in doorways and forgotten, dripping alleyways.

She shared the moment she realized her Shard's song had changed. The joyous melody of her childhood had deepened into a low, mournful hum—a constant, secret lament for her lost home, a quiet song of sorrow that only she could hear. She showed him how its power became not a tool for harmony, but for quiet survival. He felt her flinch from the violent intentions of a passing gang before they even saw her, allowing her to shrink deeper into the shadows. He felt the wave of gratitude for the rare flicker of pity that might earn her a discarded, stale piece of bread.

Finally, she let him feel the most profound ache of all: the utter, complete loneliness. The knowledge that she had no one. That her power, her light, was never a weapon to fight back, only a subtle sense that helped her endure one more day, one more cold night.

When the last memory faded, they remained at the partition, silent. Eira did not need to say anything more. She had trusted him with everything she was. And in the quiet understanding that passed between them, in the shared sorrow for the girl she had been, a new, gentle harmony began to resonate, a song only they could hear.

An oppressive security protocol had descended upon the Aurora Initiative, a silent, suffocating blanket ordered by Dr. Volkov. His personal guard, doubled in number, stood like impassive, armored statues, their presence turning the familiar corridors into a hostile gantlet. When the summons came, sharp and unavoidable, Elijah Thompson shared a look of cold dread with Maya Singh. The walk to Volkov's office felt like a final one. They checked in with the grim-faced guards, the heavy office door sealing behind them with an unnerving, definitive click.

Volkov stood behind his desk, not bothering with a pretense of welcome. The air was thick with accusation.

"Good to see you again, Adrian," Elijah began, the pleasantry sounding brittle and false even to his own ears. "How can we help?"

"There is a... discrepancy," Volkov said, his voice dangerously low, his eyes scanning them as if searching for the precise location of their lies. "A concern I am certain you can help me resolve."

"We'll certainly try," Maya offered, her own voice strained.

"The data from the Vestara expedition. The Keystone files," Volkov stated, letting the words hang in the air. "I require them. But when I attempted to access the primary archive, I found it... empty. Wiped clean. Do either of you have anything to share about this anomaly?"

Elijah's heart hammered against his ribs. He opened his mouth to offer a denial, a half-baked lie about a system glitch, anything to buy them a few more seconds.

At that exact moment, the air in the room seemed to fracture.

In the space beside Elijah's shoulder, a figure resolved itself from nothingness—a subtle, terrifying coalescence of shadow and form. Dasyra. She gently placed a hand on Elijah's shoulder, a gesture that was somehow both reassuring to him and an immense, silent threat to Volkov.

"It was my work that has veiled those files, Dr. Volkov," she said, her voice impossibly calm, yet it filled the room with an ancient authority. "They are shielded from all systems on this world, including those of your... Umbra Collective. I am Dasyra of the Bramah. This information now falls under our absolute protection."

The instant she appeared, the door burst open and Volkov's guards rushed in, weapons raised. Volkov didn't even flinch. His eyes were locked on Dasyra, his quick mind processing the impossible. With a sharp, curt motion of his hand, he dismissed them. "Stand down! Return to your posts. We are not to be disturbed again."

The guards retreated, their confusion palpable. Volkov smoothed his jacket, his composure a chilling mask over the shock. "My apologies for the crude reception, Dasyra of the Bramah. You seem to possess a great deal of knowledge about me. I, however, know almost nothing of you. Would you care to elaborate on who, precisely, the Bramah are?"

"We are the sworn guard of the Elder Gods," Dasyra stated flatly, her words landing like monoliths. "We are the instruments of cosmic Order and the arbiters of balance. We have seen empires turn to dust and stars die. Do you truly wish to test your will against ours, mortal?"

"I wouldn't dream of such a foolish action," Volkov said, his tone shifting from predator to calculating negotiator. "But might the Bramah consider that my... former... access to that data granted me insights you may not possess? Knowledge that wasn't stored on any system. Knowledge that resides only in my mind."

Dasyra's head tilted, a gesture of cold curiosity. "We are an immortal race that has witnessed the whole of history. There is nothing that hides from the Bramah."

"My knowledge regards a time *before* your creation was conceived," Volkov countered, playing his final, desperate card. "Before the gods you serve established their Order. Can the great Bramah claim to know of that time?"

A flicker of something—uncertainty? intrigue?—crossed Dasyra's serene features. "That is... impossible. Nothing came before creation's dawn."

"I believe your leaders would be very interested in what my research has uncovered," Volkov pressed, sensing the crack in her certainty. "I am willing to share it, exclusively with you. All I ask in return is the Bramah's protection from certain... inconvenient associates I have recently acquired. The Shivara."

Dasyra's eyes narrowed. "We know of your contact with the dark cult that serves them. You made a foolish pact, offered them this information, and now that it has vanished, you find yourself with a fatal debt to pay. Why should we shield you from the consequences of your own ambition?"

Volkov took a breath, laying his life on the table. "Because I can be a far more worthy asset to your needs than I could ever be to theirs. I lay my life, and my knowledge, at the mercy of the Bramah."

A long, tense silence filled the room. "So be it," Dasyra finally said, her voice a chilling verdict. "But understand this, Adrian Volkov. One failure, one hint of deception, and we will not hesitate to feed your bones to the Void ourselves."

Volkov gave a sharp, relieved nod. He turned to his private safe, retrieving two large, data-slate binders. He walked back and stood next to Dasyra, a man who had just traded one death sentence for another, more conditional one. Dasyra glanced at Elijah and Maya, a silent, unreadable acknowledgment, then placed her hand on Volkov's shoulder.

Together, they dissolved into nothingness.

Elijah and Maya stood frozen in the suddenly empty, silent office, the profound, terrifying implications of the cosmic bargain they had just witnessed washing over them.

A cold, quiet fury emanated from Kael, a pressure that made the very shadows of his sanctuary writhe. The mortal, Volkov, was late. This trivial creature, this speck of dust audacious enough to bargain with gods, had dared to test the patience of the Shivara. The contempt Kael held for the lesser races was an ancient, solid thing, and this delay was a predictable, yet infuriating, confirmation of their nature. They were creatures of chaos, distraction, and inevitable failure.

His mind, a weapon that could calcify stars, settled on a final, grim decision. Trust was a luxury, and his had been squandered.

He sent out the summons, a silent, psychic command that pierced the heart of the stronghold, a blade of pure will calling for the one instrument forged for such a task. He called for the inquisitor who could walk unseen through the fears of mortals because she had already survived the death of everything.

He called for **Vega.**

To understand the weapon Kael was about to unleash, one must understand the fire in which she was forged—a creation born of both salvation and eternal damnation.

Vega was not born Shivara. She was not created within the devouring flame at the heart of the Void. She was the sole, screaming survivor of a cosmic judgment. Eons ago, her people, a resilient race of latent psychics, had thrived on a desolate world at the frayed edge of reality. They were not powerful, but they endured. The Shivara, in their inscrutable wisdom, deemed their potential a discordant note in the grand, silent symphony of the future. Their judgment was not a war; it was an erasure. A fleet arrived, silent and absolute, and unmade her world with the cold, surgical precision of a god dissecting an insect.

In the final, agonizing moments, as her world was turning to dust and silence, the child who would become Vega did not scream or flee. She acted. Driven by a will to live that was a supernova of instinct, she wrapped her consciousness in a psychic shroud, a desperate, self-invented invisibility of the soul. She burrowed into the bedrock of her dying reality and watched, unseen, as her past, her people, and her entire existence were scoured clean from the cosmos.

Her survival was an impossibility—an anomaly that blazed like a defiant star in the perfect darkness of the Shivara's success. Kael himself, sensing this stubborn flicker of life that refused to be extinguished, took notice. He saw not a terrified orphan, but raw, defiant, *useful* potential. A tool sharp enough to be honed.

He offered her a choice that was no choice at all: perish in the silent void with the ghosts of her people, or surrender her soul to the Shivara and be reborn into a purpose worthy of her survival.

She chose purpose.

The transformation was an agony beyond mortal comprehension. In the heart of the Shivara stronghold, they took her, broke her down to her very essence, and scoured her memories clean with psychic fire. They infused her body with the chilling energies of the Void and reforged her mind in the merciless crucible of Shivara discipline and nihilism. Her name, her face, her love for her parents—all burned away, leaving only the scar tissue of a single, brutal lesson: sentiment is weakness, and survival is a weapon.

She emerged as Vega. No longer mortal, but not truly Shivara. She was something unique, something terrifying: a living weapon, her innate psychic gifts twisted and perfected into instruments of the hunt. She possesses a chilling, residual understanding of mortal fear because she has felt the ultimate measure of it. This allows her to predict her targets with flawless, predatory accuracy. But this gift is born of a deep, burning self-loathing for the weakness of her own origins, a hatred she now projects upon her prey with cold, clinical cruelty.

Her loyalty to Kael is absolute, for he is not just her master; he is her creator, the being who gave her meaning in the abyss. She is his most perfect instrument of terror, a ghost who was once a child, now unleashed to hunt down Adrian Volkov with the relentless, unforgiving focus of one who has already stared into the end of all things and survived.

She knelt before the throne of shadow, a perfect instrument of death awaiting its command, her presence a focused point of violence in the sanctuary's oppressive stillness. Kael's will, a force that could unmake stars, settled upon her.

"Vega." The name was not spoken, but impressed upon her mind, a cold and final directive. *"Your purpose is required."*

Her head lifted slightly, her eyes, burning with a cold, disciplined fire, fixed on the darkness where her master resided. Her voice was a low, resonant whisper, utterly devoid of emotion. "I am yours to command, Lord Kael. Name the target."

"Adrian Volkov," Kael's thought was sharp as obsidian. *"The mortal who had the audacity to bargain with the Shivara, and the foolishness to fail. An insult that requires correction."*

"Understood," Vega's response was immediate. A single, practical question followed, her voice chilling in its professional detachment. "Is the preservation of the target's life a required parameter for this lesson?"

A dark, cosmic amusement radiated from Kael, a feeling like the pressure of a deep-sea trench. *"His continued existence is an irrelevance. The method of his correction, the degree of his suffering... these are trivialities I leave to your discretion. I require only that the lesson be... absolute. Let your purpose be your guide, Inquisitor."*

A flicker of something that might have been satisfaction crossed Vega's face, a tightening of her lips that was more predatory than a smile.

"Then he will know the silence that consumed my world," she vowed, her voice a promise of utter annihilation. "It will be done, my Lord."

She rose in a single, fluid motion. From the shadows around her wrist, a blade of solidified Void, impossibly black and seeming to drink the faint light from the glyphs, materialized in her hand. Without another word, she turned and receded into the sanctum's gloom, a ghost of vengeance sent to introduce a foolish mortal to a fate far more terrifying than simple hellfire.

Guardians of the Keystones: Echoes

Chapter Fourteen
Aethon stood in his sanctum, the star-map a cold, indifferent swirl of galaxies. The information from Nyx was a poison, seeding doubt in the bedrock of his immortal existence. He needed more. He needed the truth from the mortal who had dared to bargain with it.

He summoned Dasyra, who materialized from the gloom like a thought given form. She bowed.

"Yes, Commander. How may I serve?"

"The debriefing of Adrian Volkov begins now," Aethon's voice was grim, devoid of its usual resolute strength. "I require the presence of Dr. Thompson and Dr. Singh from the Aurora Initiative. Their perspective may be... valuable in discerning this mortal's deceit. Retrieve them."

"At once, Commander."

Dasyra shifted into the shadows. Moments later, in Lila's sterile primary lab, she reappeared, bringing with her a bewildered and visibly tense Elijah and Maya. The air in the lab was already thick with anticipation. At Aethon's command, guards escorted Volkov into the chamber. He was unbound, but the presence of Thorne, Lila, and Dasyra, positioned like silent, ancient monoliths, was a more effective cage than any energy field.

Aethon's gaze was like the weight of a dying star. "You have bargained for your life with the promise of knowledge, Adrian Volkov. Present this information now. Prove that you are worthy of the protection of the Bramah.”

Volkov met the ancient commander’s gaze, a flicker of audacious confidence in his eyes. “My work with the Umbra Collective uncovered a truth more fundamental than your Order seems to comprehend. The power crystals your people call Keystones… they pre-date your gods.”

The Bramah in the room remained perfectly still, but a palpable shockwave, a psychic tremor, emanated from Aethon.

Volkov pressed his advantage, his voice low and compelling. “They were not merely tools used to create universes. They were forged by beings of such power that your gods would be but fleeting sparks in comparison. It is even possible that these beings… created your gods as well. That is the truth I offer.”

“Blasphemy!” The word ripped from Aethon’s throat, a raw, guttural sound of pure outrage that shattered his millennia of composure. “There is nothing more powerful than the Gods! They are the beginning and the end!”

“Perhaps not now,” Volkov countered calmly. “But what of the time before? That is all the truth I currently possess.”

“Impossible!” Aethon roared, his fists clenched, the foundations of his faith cracking. “The Gods have *always* been! Nothing precedes them!” He turned abruptly, his great cloak swirling. “Thorne, continue the interrogation.” His voice was a strained command. “I must… contemplate.”

He strode from the lab, his exit not one of fury, but of a being in profound, existential crisis, desperately seeking solitude to prevent his own unraveling from being witnessed.

A tense silence filled the room, broken only by Elijah, who stepped forward, his expression a mask of cold, suspicious anger. He was no longer a scientist in the presence of a superior; he was a man betrayed.

“Let’s talk about something more recent, Volkov,” Elijah’s voice was sharp as surgical steel. “When did the Umbra Collective sink its claws into the Aurora Initiative? How deep does the rot go?”

A slow, cynical smile spread across Volkov's face. He seemed to relish the change in topic, the chance to detail his victory. "Ah, the noble Dr. Thompson. Still clinging to the dream." He began to speak, his tone a mocking lecture. He told them everything—of the Initiative's hopeful, naive founding by the visionary Dr. Aris Sterling, a dream of shared knowledge for the betterment of all. He then described how his own ancient, secretive Collective saw this beacon of hope not as an inspiration, but as the perfect, unsuspecting host.

"You have to understand," Volkov said, looking from Elijah to Maya, enjoying their dawning horror, "your Initiative's greatest successes were our greatest triumphs. A new medical breakthrough? A gift from a forgotten alien text in our archives. A new engine design? Reverse-engineered from a derelict ship we found on a mission *you* funded. We gave you miracles to keep your reputation pristine, and in return, you gave us the keys to the kingdom—labs, ships, resources... and your absolute, trusting ignorance."

"So, it was all a lie," Maya whispered, her voice trembling with disillusionment. "All of it."

"Not a lie, Dr. Singh," Volkov corrected her, his smile widening. "A symbiotic relationship. You provided the body. We provided the soul." He leaned forward, his voice dropping to a final, chilling whisper that seemed meant for them alone. "The Aurora Initiative you loved died long ago. You've just been living in its beautiful, well-funded corpse. My only mistake was trying to elevate us to the divine. Now, the real question for you both is... with me gone... who do you think is in charge of it *now*?"

The guards returned Volkov to his sterile cell deep within the stronghold. He heard the magnetic lock hiss shut, and a smirk played on his lips. He had done it. He had played gods and monsters against each other and secured his own survival. The fools. The Bramah were his shields now. He was safe. He kicked his feet back on his cot, the picture of arrogant repose.

But the air in the cell began to change. A subtle drop in temperature, sharp and sudden. A thin, cold mist, smelling of ozone and ancient, forgotten dust, began to seep from the ventilation grate, pooling on the floor and clinging to it like a burial shroud. Volkov sat up, his smirk vanishing, replaced by a flicker of confusion that quickly curdled into alarm.

From the heart of the coiling mist, a form resolved itself—Vega. Her eyes burned with a cold fire that promised nothing but endings.

Before Volkov could even draw breath to shout, she was upon him. It was not a rush, but a glide, a silent flow of chilling purpose. The hilt of her Void blade struck the base of his neck with surgical precision, sending a wave of icy paralysis through his limbs. He crumpled to the floor, his mouth open in a silent scream that would never find voice.

She knelt beside him, her movements unnervingly graceful, and pressed a single, cold finger to his lips. "Shhh," she whispered, her voice a poisonously gentle rustle. "Now, now, Adrian. Let's not allow alarms to interrupt our... reunion. It seems you forgot your debt to the Shivara. You forgot the gravity of your promise to Lord Kael. And now we must meet under such... difficult circumstances."

Terror flared in Volkov's paralyzed eyes. His mind raced, desperate. *"I... I'm sorry!"* he tried to project, his voice a frantic mental shriek. *"I was captured by the Bramah! I was going to break out and come to you as we agreed!"*

Vega's head tilted, a gesture of almost scientific curiosity at the pathetic lie. "Really, Adrian?" her voice was a low, mocking purr. "What sort of fool do you imagine you are dealing with? A child who believes such facile tales?"

"I can get the data! Soon! I just need more time!"

"I'm afraid your time is a currency you have already spent," Vega said, her voice losing all pretense of gentleness, becoming as cold and absolute as the Void itself. "The bill is due. And since you do not have the data... your life is the payment."

The fear in Volkov's face deepened into something far beyond mortal terror as Vega placed her cold palm against his forehead. "You failed to deliver knowledge," she whispered, her eyes beginning to glow with a faint, terrible light. "So I shall gift you some of my own."

And then, she pushed.

She didn't just break past his mental shields; she shattered them into psychic shrapnel. She poured the memory of her world's death directly into his consciousness. Volkov's mind was flooded, drowned in the psychic shriek of a billion souls dying at once. He saw a sky torn open to reveal a silent, judging fleet. He felt the ground beneath his feet not shake, but cease to exist. He felt the love for his own parents, his own people, rise up only to be scoured away by a wave of absolute, methodical erasure. He was subjected to the final, agonizing moments of her entire race, and then, the most terrible part: the soul-crushing, eternal, planet-sized silence of being the only one left.

Volkov's mind, unable to process the sheer scale of the alien grief, the second hand trauma, and the cosmic loneliness, simply... ended. It did not break; it was annihilated, his consciousness erased like a flawed equation.

Vega withdrew her hand from the twitching, empty husk that was once an ambitious man. There was no satisfaction on her face, no triumph, only the quiet finality of a debt collected. She straightened up, and without a sound, dissolved back into the lingering mist. The mist, in turn, slowly dissipated, leaving the cell pristine, silent, and forever haunted by a horror it could not contain.

The air in Lila's primary lab, usually a place of quiet, sterile contemplation, was electric with the thrill of discovery. Elijah Thompson, leaning over a holographic display, felt a sense of awe that momentarily eclipsed his deep-seated paranoia. Beside him, Lila was orchestrating a symphony of data, translating the raw, impossible knowledge from Volkov's binders into patterns the Bramah's analytic core could begin to process.

"The structural consistency... it's unlike any physics I've ever encountered," Elijah murmured, tracing a complex molecular diagram with his finger. "It suggests a state of matter from a universe with entirely different fundamental laws."

"Or from a universe before such laws were written," Lila countered, her eyes alight with a fervent, intellectual fire. "We are looking at the blueprint of a time before time, Elijah. This is..."

Her words were cut short. Two Bramah guards, members of the elite stronghold sentinels, appeared at the lab's entrance. Their usual stoic calm was gone, replaced by a grim, palpable tension that instantly soured the atmosphere of discovery. They approached Thorne, who stood observing the work, and spoke in low, hushed tones, but Elijah was close enough to catch chilling fragments: *"...no vital signs... cell is pristine... as if he just... stopped."*

Elijah saw Thorne's entire posture go rigid, his face hardening into a mask of cold fury. Without a word to Lila or Elijah, he spun on his heel, his armored boots striking the deck plates with sharp, angry purpose as he strode from the lab. His mind raced, each step a hammer blow of failure. *The stronghold. Breached. The asset. Terminated. Under my watch.* The thought was a shard of ice in his gut. The threat to Eira and Erebus was no longer theoretical; it was now a living, breathing presence within their walls.

He didn't request an audience; he burst into Aethon's command sanctum. The commander was standing before the grand star-map, lost in contemplation, the weight of Nyx's divine warning visible in his somber stance.

"Commander!" Thorne's voice was a sharp crack in the chamber's quiet solemnity, pulling Aethon from his thoughts. "A critical security failure. The asset, Adrian Volkov—he's dead. He was eliminated in his secure cell."

Aethon turned slowly, his face a storm cloud of cold fury and disbelief. The sanctity of their home, their most sacred bastion, had been violated with contemptuous ease. "How?" The word was a low growl, filled with a dangerous pressure that seemed to make the air vibrate. "Report. Every detail."

"There is little to report," Thorne said, his voice tight with controlled frustration. "There are no signs of forced entry. No alarms were triggered, no energy signatures logged. He was simply... extinguished. The guards found him moments ago. It's as if his life was surgically removed from his body." He paused, the grim conclusion unavoidable. "The method was too clean, too silent. We believe it to be the work of Vega, the Shivara Inquisitor. Her abilities are the only logical explanation for a breach this absolute."

"Damn it!" Aethon slammed a gauntleted fist onto his command console, the crack of the impact echoing the shattering of their security. He stared at the star-map, but the swirling galaxies now seemed to mock him, a vast, indifferent wilderness where his fortress was no better than a tent in a hurricane. "A ghost. A ghost in our own home. She walks our halls at will, and we are blind to her presence." He fixed Thorne with an intense, burning stare. "Did we get anything from him before his... expiration? Was this entire, dangerous bargain for nothing?"

"We acquired the primary data he offered, Commander," Thorne confirmed. "The information from the binders Lila and Dr. Thompson are now processing. It yielded a set of coordinates, pointing to a location in uncharted space, deep within a shroud nebula." He added, his tone laced with suspicion, "We have no way of knowing if it's the profound truth he promised, or a final, posthumous trap laid by the Shivara to lure us out."

"So he gives us a potential key with one hand, while the Shivara take his life with the other," Aethon mused, his voice a low rumble of frustration. "This reeks of manipulation. This changes the parameters of everything." He paced the sanctum, the leader's mind processing the new, terrifying variables. "I must seek guidance from the Elder Gods directly.

Their wisdom is needed to navigate this treacherous fog." He stopped, his gaze sharp and decisive.

"Your orders, Commander?" Thorne asked, ready for action.

"Your primary duty remains with Lila and the data. Whatever those coordinates point to, the information we gathered at Elyria may be the only key to understanding it safely. But first," Aethon's voice became grave, "return Dr. Thompson and Dr. Singh to the Aurora Initiative, effective immediately. They came here believing they were our colleagues; they cannot remain as targets. They are no longer safe here. If Vega can get to Volkov in a secured cell, she can get to them. Provide them with a full security detail for the transit and ensure their safety upon return."

He took a breath, his command ringing with new urgency. "And Thorne—raise security protocols across the entire stronghold to level five. Activate the Chronos Wards. I want every corridor, every shadow, under temporal surveillance. We must find a way to see this ghost. We must find a way to stop Vega before she decides to hunt a more valuable target."

"It will be done, Commander." Thorne acknowledged, turning to carry out the commands, the weight of their new reality—that the war was no longer just outside their walls, but had already slipped, silent and unseen, within them—settling heavily upon him.

Upon their covert return to the Aurora Initiative, a palpable urgency propelled Elijah and Maya directly to Volkov's now-vacant office. The air itself seemed to hum with suppressed secrets, a stark contrast to the sterile quiet of the space. Elijah's gaze swept over the meticulously arranged desk, his mind already racing.

"Maya," Elijah's voice was a low, urgent murmur, barely above a whisper. "We need to locate anything, *anything* of value, before the Umbra Collective realizes Adrian is gone. They'll scour this place clean, erase every trace of his work." His words were heavy with the unspoken threat of their enemies' swift retaliation.

Maya's eyes, usually bright with curiosity, were now shadowed with apprehension. "Do you think the Shivara might come after us next? They know we were with Volkov."

Elijah paused, considering the chilling possibility. "Possibly. The universe is shifting beneath our feet, and their motives are as inscrutable as ever. But we can't afford to focus on that right now. The first order of business, our immediate priority, is securing as much data as we possibly can from this office. The second will be a far more daunting task: systematically ridding the Initiative of any lingering influence from the Umbra Collective."

Maya's gaze flickered around the imposing office, a daunting task indeed. "I don't even know where to begin with that, Elijah. Who can we truly trust? How will we ever know who's compromised?" Her voice was laced with a deep-seated concern that mirrored his own.

"One thing at a time, Maya," Elijah reiterated, his tone a quiet reassurance that belied the turmoil within him.

Hours bled into a blur of meticulous searching. They painstakingly sifted through Volkov's records, a veritable labyrinth of encrypted files and physical documents, saving every scrap of information they deemed vital into several hidden folders. Elijah then retrieved the peculiar device loaned to him by Dasrya, its surface cool and smooth beneath his fingertips. With precise, practiced movements, he used it to veil the newly secured files deep within the Initiative's system, cloaking them in layers of digital shadow for greater security.

It was amidst this digital excavation that a name began to surface with alarming regularity: Nalini Sharma. Volkov had clearly been highly interested in her, her name repeated several times in his private notes, always accompanied by a cryptic notation about her "abilities." Beyond that, nothing else was listed, no hint as to the nature of these abilities or why she had captivated the attention of a man deeply entrenched in the Umbra Collective. Elijah's gut instinct, a sensation that rarely led him astray, told him that Nalini Sharma was their next, crucial target. They had to reach her before the Collective did.

A rapid search through city records yielded her official designation: Civic Data Archivist for the Acarcis municipal division. It was an innocuous, almost mundane title, yet it clashed violently with Volkov's intense interest. What hidden potential lay within a mere archivist that would draw the attention of such a dangerous organization? The question gnawed at Elijah, fueling his sense of urgency.

With their destination set, Elijah and Maya made their way to the bustling government sector of the city. They navigated the labyrinthine corridors, a sea of bustling government employees, most too engrossed in their work to even notice the two figures moving with quiet purpose through the massive, echoing rooms. They eventually located her division, and then, nestled within a vast expanse of common terminals, a small, unassuming office. Elijah's heart quickened as he quietly pressed the buzzer on the door. It opened swiftly, revealing a young woman, her brow furrowed in concentration, diligently at work at a common terminal.

"Are you Nalini Sharma?" Elijah inquired, his voice carefully neutral, a practiced veneer of officialdom.

Her eyes, sharp and intelligent, met his. "Yes. How can I help you?" Her tone was calm, betraying no surprise.

"I am Dr. Elijah Thompson," he began, offering a slight, deferential nod, "and this is Dr. Maya Singh. We are from the **Aurora Initiative**. We need to speak with you in private, if possible. It's... a matter of considerable importance."

A faint, knowing smile touched Nalini's lips, a flicker of something ancient in her gaze that sent a shiver down Elijah's spine. "You are the others," she stated, not as a question, but as a quiet affirmation. "I know of you both. Yes, let's take a stroll."

She rose fluidly, a quiet grace in her movements. Retrieving a set of keys, she locked her office door with a soft click and began walking down a short, nondescript corridor towards an exit. As they emerged into a large, sun-drenched courtyard, the warmth of the light felt strangely at odds with the deepening mystery. Elijah, a man who prided himself on understanding the complexities of the universe, found himself utterly bewildered by her words.

"What did you mean by 'others', Nalini?" Elijah pressed, his confusion outweighing his usual caution. "How do you know us?"

Nalini turned to face them, her expression serene, yet profound. "I saw you in a vision," she explained, her voice soft but unwavering. "You, too, perceive that this world isn't right, that it has been... altered. You are the only ones, other than myself, who seem to remember the truth."

"A *vision*?" Maya interrupted, her skepticism momentarily overriding her usual composure.

"Yes," Nalini affirmed, her gaze distant, as if seeing beyond the present moment. "I could vividly see this world change, shift, to what it is now. Many things were profoundly different before. You've seen this too, haven't you?" Her question held a quiet knowing, a shared secret.

Elijah and Maya exchanged a glance. "Yes," Elijah admitted, the word a reluctant confession. "We have. Do you understand why? Do you know what caused it?"

A hint of wistfulness entered Nalini's voice. "I saw many things in my vision that I couldn't fully comprehend, fragments of a greater truth. But it seemed to be a dimensional shift, somehow. A profound alteration of reality. I don't know what caused it, or who. Only that it happened."

Elijah knew, instinctively, that they had found someone truly extraordinary. "Would you be willing to return to the Aurora Initiative with us, Nalini?" he asked, his voice now imbued with a hopeful urgency. "We believe we might be able to explain some things to you. Things that might connect with what you've seen."

Nalini met his gaze, a quiet understanding passing between them. A future, uncertain but undeniably linked, stretched before them. "Yes," she simply stated, her single word a silent promise of alliance in a world now shrouded in profound mystery and hidden threats.

Eira and Erebus sat, fidgeting with a restless energy, watching the frenetic bustle of activity around them. They were confined, yet acutely aware of the deep anxieties gripping the Bramah. They were consumed by the sudden, unsettling silence from the Elder Gods, their usual guidance was once again utterly absent. The cosmic tremors, the baffling behavior of the Shivara, and the cryptic, incomplete data salvaged from Volkov's hidden files had thrown the entire stronghold into a state of heightened alert and frantic investigation. There was so little for Eira and Erebus to do but observe, and boredom, it seemed, was a powerful catalyst for nascent power.

A spark of daring curiosity ignited in Eira's mind. *What else could she do?* She closed her eyes, focusing intently on the far corner of her enclosure, a simple, daring thought forming: *be there.* The world seemed to stretch, then snap back with a disorienting lurch, and in a flash of pure exhilaration, she was standing on the other side of the room. A breathless, ecstatic laugh escaped her.

"Erebus! Did you see that?!" she shrieked, her voice bubbling with incredulous delight. "We can transport! We can just... go! Who knows how far this works!"

Erebus, whose eyes had widened in astonishment at her sudden disappearance and reappearance, felt an electrifying surge. "What?! Let me try!" He squeezed his eyes shut, concentrating with fierce intent on the opposite wall of his room. A split-second later, with a similar jolt, he had relocated. A wide, unburdened grin split his face. "This is incredible! Come on, Eira! Let's see how far we can go!"

The carefully designed confines of their enclosures, then the specialized laboratory, quickly dissolved into a dizzying blur. Within seconds, they were shifting around the lab, appearing and disappearing in bursts of displaced air. The thrill of it was intoxicating. Then, with a shared, reckless impulse, they found themselves beyond the contained areas, deep within the Bramah stronghold itself. Immediately, blaring sirens shattered the air, painting the corridors with urgent, flashing red lights, each pulse a testament to the Bramah's heightened security protocols already strained by the divine silence. But Eira and Erebus paid it little attention, their laughter echoing through the cavernous halls. They were having too much exhilarating fun to stop, drunk on this sudden, boundless freedom.

Lila and Thorne, their faces a mask of growing alarm, rushed to locate them, their own internal readouts confirming impossible energy signatures. Each time they pinpointed the mischievous pair, Eira and Erebus would flash to another location, turning the Bramah's advanced surveillance into a frustrating game of cosmic hide-and-seek. They dissolved and reappeared, their joyful shouts echoing, reveling in their fleeting liberation.

"I wonder if we can go to another place entirely?" Eira's thought pulsed to Erebus, a tantalizing invitation. She immediately had a place in mind—a vivid, almost haunting image from a brief, unexplained memory. It was a place of breathtaking beauty. She looked at Erebus, her eyes shining with a potent mixture of desire and daring. "Focus on this, Erebus," she urged, sending the image directly into his consciousness: a vast, undulating field of shimmering silver grass, dancing under the benevolent glow of two distant suns. A silent, reckless agreement passed between them. In a blink, reality warped, stretched, and then snapped back into place.

They were standing on Vestara, just outside the mythical, lost city of Elyria. The air was cool and sweet, scented with alien flora, and the melodic, otherworldly song of the echo weavers drifted on the breeze. The silver grass, just as Eira had imagined, shimmered like liquid moonlight under the gentle light of the twin suns beginning their descent.

Back in the stronghold, Lila and Thorne stared at the impossible reading on the primary locator. Their two charges, their precious, powerful charges, had not merely breached containment; they had left the stronghold entirely. Lila's fingers flew across the console, running frantic calculations, desperate to understand the impossible jump. Her face paled as the results flashed: *Vestara*. Her heart seized with a cold dread. This wasn't just a security breach; it was a cosmic anomaly, precisely what the Bramah feared in the wake of the gods' silence and Volkov's unsettling data.

She spun to Thorne, her voice tight with grave concern. "We need to get them back in their enclosures immediately. And make them understand the absolute, critical importance of staying there. If they have these abilities, if this is connected to what the Keystones are doing, if this is what Volkov was looking for... the implications are catastrophic."

Thorne, his jaw clenched, was already moving towards the transport bay, overriding safety protocols. "Inform Aethon of the situation, Lila. Tell him I'm going to retrieve them myself. Now. We can't risk them falling into the wrong hands with power like this."

On Vestara, oblivious to the panic they had caused, Eira and Erebus were bathed in the ethereal glow of the twin suns' setting. The sky was a breathtaking canvas of deep blues, fiery reds, and molten golds, washing over the silver plains in a spectacle of unparalleled beauty. Erebus, his heart swelling with a warmth he'd never known, slowly, tentatively, put his arm around Eira. She leaned into his touch, a sigh escaping her lips.

"I love you, Eira," he whispered, the words raw and true, foreign on his tongue yet utterly right. "I... I never knew these feelings existed before you."

She smiled, a pure, incandescent joy lighting her face, and looked deeply into his eyes, her own emotions mirroring his. He lowered his head, and their lips met in a tender, hesitant kiss, a universe of new sensations blossoming between them. In that precious, suspended moment, Eira felt the exquisite bliss of his embrace, a profound connection that anchored her in a swirling reality. Yet, even as their lips met, a subtle, anxious tremor ran through her. She knew, with an intuitive certainty, that their time together like this, stolen and sweet, was running out. But she wanted to savor every fleeting second, to commit this feeling, this *love*, to every fiber of her being. She had never felt such warmth, such protective tenderness.

Suddenly, a distant figure emerged from the shimmering silver grass, running, a frantic blur. It was Thorne, his shouts carried on the wind, begging them, pleading with them, to move apart immediately. *But was he too late?*

At the very center of Elyria's Citadel, deep within its forgotten core, the Resonant Orb pulsed to life, a faint, internal light blossoming within its ancient crystalline shell. The pulses quickened over time, each beat echoing the one before it, growing in intensity. And in its hidden chamber beneath, the Prime Keystone began to glow, its dormant power stirring with a profound awakening. The Orb and the Keystone pulsed together, like a single, colossal heart beginning to beat after an eternity of slumber, its rhythm resonating with the cosmic tremors felt across the multiverse. On the surface, there was a low-pitched hum that got louder, deeper, more pervasive with each passing second, vibrating through the very ground. As Thorne finally closed the distance, his face contorted in a desperate plea, he screamed for them to stand apart.

Shocked by his raw terror, by the sudden, overwhelming hum that permeated everything, Eira and Erebus instinctively did as they were told, stumbling away from each other just as the humming reached a deafening crescendo. The winds seemed to die, utterly. The very air grew heavy, still. The planet itself seemed to hold its breath. Then, everything went completely, terrifyingly silent. No wind. No melodic song of the echo weavers. Just pure, absolute quiet, a void of sound that pressed in on their ears, their very souls.

Then, from nowhere and everywhere, a voice, ancient and resonant, a force of nature given utterance, boomed into existence, echoing through the newfound stillness of the universe.

"Release me!"

Pronunciations

- Aethon - (A-thon)
- Arkeia - (Ark-e-a)
- Asphodel - (As-fo-del)
- Dasyra - (Das-ira)
- Eira - (I-ra)
- Erebus - (Er-ibus)
- Kael - (Kale)
- Imperatrix - (Im-per-ra-triks)
- Niamh - (Neme)

15

Acknowledgments

First, I thank God for blessing me with this book. I've wanted to do justice to this story, and I hope I do so in this series.
Thank you to my angel, my life, Melissa.
To my son and daughter-in-law, James and Anna.
Thanks, Anna, for the artwork!
To my brother, Rick.
For the encouragement from my friends, Kelly, Raychel, and so many others.
To all those that enjoy this series, especially the first readers.
Lastly, to my little Kibbles, who flew over the rainbow bridge in May of 2017. I still miss you and hope to see you again one day.

Ed's Bio

After 61 years of accumulating life experience, Ed Morgan decided it was finally time to write a book, mostly to prove to his family what he's been muttering about in the corner. His expertise is eclectic: he can tell you the life story of a cockatoo and also capture its good side on camera, as he is both a parrot expert and a photographer.

He shares his life with his wife, Melissa, a saint who has graciously tolerated years of plot-related mumbling and the occasional squawk from his co-authors (the parrots). Ed's writing process is fueled by coffee, curiosity, and the constant threat of a parrot stealing his keyboard. He has a son, James, who is just grateful his father decided to write fantasy books instead of training an army of birds to reenact them. Finally, there is Bailey, the dog, who works as business manager and financial planner. He prefers all money be put towards treats and toys to rip apart in less than five minutes flat.